Thomas F. Hill

Antient Erse Poems

Collected among the Scottish Highlands, in order to illustrate the Ossian of

Mr. Macpherson

Thomas F. Hill

Antient Erse Poems
Collected among the Scottish Highlands, in order to illustrate the Ossian of Mr. Macpherson

ISBN/EAN: 9783337238872

Printed in Europe, USA, Canada, Australia, Japan

Cover: Foto ©Andreas Hilbeck / pixelio.de

More available books at **www.hansebooks.com**

ANTIENT ERSE POEMS,

COLLECTED AMONG THE

SCOTTISH HIGHLANDS,

IN ORDER TO ILLUSTRATE THE

OSSIAN OF MR. MACPHERSON.

EDINBURGH:

MACLACHLAN & STEWART, 64 SOUTH BRIDGE.

1878.

THE following Poems were first published during the Years 1782 and 1783 in THE GENTLEMAN'S MAGAZINE; a Periodical Publication of considerable note in the Annals of British Literature.

[In 1784 it was published in Pamphlet form, from which this Edition is reprinted.]

ANTIENT ERSE POEMS.

TO THE EDITORS OF THE GENTLEMAN'S MAGAZINE.

THE controversy about Ossian having been lately revived, both in the newspapers, and separate pamphlets, as well as in your Magazine; not without the intervention of several respectable names; I take the liberty of troubling you with some facts relative to it, which I obtained in an excursion of some months through the Highlands in the summer of the year 1780. I should scarcely have thought them worthy of the public attention, if the subject had not been revived with so much ardour; though they seem to me capable of affording much additional, and even new light. If your opinion of them agrees with mine, I shall be happy to see them inserted among your valuable collections.

It had ever appeared to me, that the arguments on both sides of this dispute, were attended with particular obscurity. The supporters of the authenticity of the Ossian of Mr. Macpherson, have been either unable or unwilling, to produce the authorities they pretend to. The antagonists of this opinion, on the other hand, though they cannot deny the existence of peculiar traditional and historic songs in the Highlands, and though they boast of invincible proofs that Mr. Macpherson's Ossian is wholly a forgery, and not copied from any such songs, yet even the great Dr. Johnson himself has no claim to any knowledge of those songs. From such considerations, I was induced to believe, that the subject might be considerably elucidated, by collecting these songs in their original form : and I therefore made it a part of my business, during my journey through the Highlands, to search out the traditionary preservers of them, and procure copies with as much attention and exactness as lay in the power of a foreigner, and a stranger to the language. The absurd difficulties I had to encounter with in this pursuit it is not necessary to enumerate : sometimes I was obliged to dissemble a knowledge of the Erse, of which I scarcely understood six words ; sometimes I was forced to assume the character of a profest author, zealous to defend the honour of Ossian and Mr. Macpherson. It is not, however, impertinent to remark, that after I had obtained written copies in Erse of several of the following songs, I found it very difficult to get them translated ; for though many understand Erse as a speech, few are yet acquainted with it as a written language.*

* *Vide* Dr. Johnson's Tour to the Hebrides.

Before I proceed any further, it appears to me requisite, for the clear understanding of what follows, to remark that the dispute seems naturally to divide itself into three questions : first, Whether the Ossian of Mr. Macpherson be really the production of a very ancient Highland bard, called by that name? or, secondly, Whether it be copied from old songs, preserved indeed in the Highlands, but written by unknown bards, and only doubtfully and traditionally ascribed to Ossian? or, If it be wholly a forgery of Mr. Macpherson's?

Considerable opportunities were afforded me, towards obtaining information on these heads, by three several tours which I made in the Highlands. The first of these lay through the internal parts of that country, from Edinburgh to Perth, Dunkeld, Blair in Athole, Tay-mouth, Dalmaly in Glenorchy, Inverara, Loch-Lomond, Dunbarton, Glasgow, Hamilton, and Lanerk. In this tour I was honoured with the company of J. Stokes, M.D., of Worcester, now on his travels abroad,* but then a student at Edinburgh, a gentleman eminent for his literary abilities, and a strenuous unbeliever in Ossian. From Lanerk I crost to Linlithgow, Sterling, Perth, Forfar, Brechyn, Stonehaven, Aberdeen, Strath-Spey, Elgin, and Inverness, travelling along the eastern coast, or Lowlands, as they are called. From Inverness I proceeded along the military roads, down the Lakes, by Fort Augustus, to Fort William ; and still pursuing the military road, crost over the Black Mountain to Tiendrum. In this stage I visited Glen-Co, famous in Scotland for its romantic scenery, for the massacre which happened there soon after the Revolution, and also for being one of the habitations assigned by tradition to Ossian.

Leaving Tiendrum a second time, I returned by Loch-Ern, Dumblaine, and Alloa, to Edinburgh.

Such was the direction of my two first tours through the Highlands : the third, in which I was happy enough to procure far the greater number of the following songs, led me from Edinburgh, through Sterling and Callender, by the Head of Loch-Ern, to Tiendrum for the third, and Dalmaly for the second time. From Dalmaly I went by Loch-Etive, to Oban, where I took boat for Mull, and spent near a fortnight in the Western Isles ; visiting Staffa, and Icolmkill ; and Morven on the mainland. In my return from Oban, I crost over to Loch-Aw, Inverara, Loch-Lomond, Dunbarton, and Glasgow ; thus finishing my wanderings among the Alps of our Island. I think it necessary thus to delineate the track I pursued ; that I may remove every doubt respecting the evidence I am about to produce ; as I shall have occasion to refer hereafter to the different stages of my journey.

In the course of these researches I found that although every district had its own peculiar historic songs, yet the inhabitants of one valley were scarcely acquainted with those which were current in the next. The songs relating to the Feinne, and their chieftain, Fion-mac-Coul, or Fion-na-Gaël, whom we call in English Fingal, are wholly confined to Argyleshire and the Western Highlands, where the scene of their actions is supposed to have lain. In that district almost every one is acquainted with them ; and all whose situation in life enables them to become acquainted with the subject, are zealous assertors of the authenticity of the Ossian of Mr. Mac-

* In the year 1782. Dr. Stokes is now settled at Kidderminster in Worcestershire.

pherson. Yet it is remarkable, that I never could meet with Mr. Macpherson's work in any part of the Highlands; and many of his defenders confessed that they had never seen it. The only book I met with, which had any immediate connection with it, was Mr. Hole's poetic version of Fingal, which I saw at Mr. Macleane's, of Drumnan in Morven. I do not mean, however, to tax any of Ossian's Highland partizans with direct falsehood; they have all heard that the stories of Mr. Macpherson relate to Fingal and his heroes; they themselves have also often heard songs relating to the same people, and ascribed to Ossian. On this loose basis, I fear, their testimonies often rest.

The first song relating to the Feinne, which I procured in the Highlands, was obtained from a native of Argyleshire, who was gardener to the Duke of Athol at Dunkeld. Its subject is humourous, and even ridiculous; for Fingal is not always treated with respect in the Highlands, any more than our King Arthur in the old ballads of this country. A taylor happening to come to Fingal's habitation, found the heroes in such need of his art, that they began quarrelling about precedence, every hero wanting his own clothes made first; Dermid, particularly, proceeded even to blows in support of his claim. By this means the whole host of the Feinne, or Fingalians, was thrown into confusion; till at length, an old hero restored peace, by persuading them to turn out the taylor: which expedient was adopted, and Fingal's heroes determined to wear their old clothes a little longer.

Mr. Stuart, minister of Blair, whom I also visited in company with Mr. Stokes, was the only person I met with in the Highlands who expressed any doubts respecting Mr. Macpherson's Ossian. Mr. Stuart told us, that there were indeed many songs preserved in Argyleshire, and the Western Highlands, under the name of Ossian, relating to Fingal and his heroes: "but," says he, "we have our doubts with regard to Mr. Macpherson's poems, because he has not published the originals."

Mr. Stuart favoured us with the story of a song, relating to Dermid, one of the Feinne, who had raised Fingal's jealousy by too great an intimacy with his wife. Fingal in revenge, having determined to destroy Dermid, took the opportunity of putting his purpose in execution, by means of a boar which had been slain in one of their huntings. It was a notion in those times, Mr. Stuart added, that walking along the back of a boar, in a direction contrary to the bristles, was certain death. Fingal commanded Dermid to do this, and by that means put an end to his life. I afterwards obtained a copy of this song in the original Erse; Mr. Smith also, the editor of a late collection of Ossian's poems,* has inserted a copy of it; they both differ in many circumstances from the foregoing account; Mr. Smith's likewise is much longer and more correct.

By the assistance of Mr. Stuart, I was afterwards directed to one James Maclauchlan, a very old man, much celebrated for his knowledge of ancient songs. Maclauchlan was a taylor; those artists being of all men the most famous for this qualification.† I found him in an old woman's cottage,

---

* *Galic Antiquities* published that very year, 1780, at Edinburgh.

† Taylors, in Scotland and the North of England, work in the houses of their employers; and their songs serve for the entertainment, both of themselves and their hosts, during their labour.

near Blair, entirely willing to gratify my curiosity, and indeed highly flattered that I paid so much attention to his songs : but as he could not talk English, I was obliged to supply myself with another cottager, to translate whilst he sung. The following poem I wrote down from the mouth of our interpreter ; a circumstance which naturally accounts for the ruggedness of the language : the good old woman, who sat by spinning, assured me, that, if I had understood the original, it would have drawn tears from my eyes. The poem is an elegy on a gentleman of the clan of MacGregor, who died in the prime of life : the author mourns over his deceased patron himself, and describes the sorrow of the rest of his friends : I have some reasons to believe it was published in the original Erse, by Mr. MacDonald, in a collection of Erse poems printed at Edinburgh about eight or ten years ago.

"The sighs of my heart vex me sore ; the sight of my eyes is not good ; it has raised my sorrows, and doubled my tears ; the man of Doonan is not alive ; there are many gentlemen making his bed, and their sorrow is dropping on their shoes : his mistress is, as it were, crucified for his love.—It is no wonder she should be sorrowful, for she shall never get such another after him. When I would sit by myself (and consider) the like of him was not to be gotten with or without riches. His heart was raised up, his fiddle at your ear, and his pipes playing about your town. When he would sit down, he heard the sound of his cups ; and his servants serving him while he was at rest.—It is the meaning of my words ; how many worthy men, who have been great drinkers have died. Of them were Alexander Rowey, and Black John of strong Arms ; I think them far off from me without life.—You were the chief of the people, going far before them, and a good lord of your tenants at home. When you took your arms, they did not rust ; every hunting you made there was blood. You got honour going before them, and although you got more than they, you were worthy of it." I will never walk West on the road to the (peat) stack any more, for I have lost my mirth and the laird of Reanach." †

As I had been informed, in my first excursion through the Highlands, that one Mac-Nab, a blacksmith at Dalmaly, had made it his business to collect and copy many of the songs attributed to Ossian : I determined upon revisiting Dalmaly, in order to obtain from him all the intelligence he was able to afford me. He lives in a cottage, not far from the inn and church at Dalmaly, where he boasts that his ancestors have been blacksmiths for near 400 years; and where also he preserves, with much respect, the coat-armour of the blacksmiths his forefathers. I found him by no means deficient in ingenuity. A blacksmith in the Highlands is a more respectable character than with us in England. He is referred to by Mr. Smith, above-mentioned, as one of his authorities, for the Erse poems he has published ; a circumstance which may perhaps diminish the validity of his testimony, with some of the zealous antagonists of Ossian ; ‡ but, as the poems he favoured me with have little agreement with those published by Macpherson and Smith, I think the force of prejudice alone can persuade us to refuse

---

* At this place, we suspected that our interpreter, weary of his employment, desired old Maclauchlan to omit a considerable part of the song, and repeat the concluding verse immediately.

† Reanach is, I believe, in Athol, not far from Glen Lion, where a branch of the Tay flows through a lake of that name.

‡ Galic Antiq. Edinbur. 1780, p. 128, note. Mac-Nab himself mentioned this to me, and seemed much pleased that his name was in print.

it.* I have reason to believe that Mac-Nab had never read the Ossian of Mr. Macpherson.

From this man I obtained many Songs, which are traditionally ascribed to Ossian. The following Poem of *Ossian agus an Clerich*, he gave me in Erse ; for to him I pretended a knowledge in that language. I had it afterwards translated by Mr. Darrach, a gentleman who lived with Mr. Maclean, of Scallastel in Mull, as tutor to his children, and who was wholly unacquainted with Mac-Nab. I set down the translation in the rude form it received from immediate verbal composition. It differs in chronology from the Poems of Ossian already published ; representing that bard as the contemporary of St. Patrick ; agreeable to a tradition which I found very prevalent in Argyleshire ; according to which St. Patrick was Ossian's son-in-law. The Poem is a dialogue between St. Patrick the *Clerich* or *Clerk*, and Ossian.

OSSIAN AGUS AN CLERICH.

OSSHIAN. 1.
A Clerich achanfas na Sailm
Air leom fein gur borb do Chial
Nach eist thu Tamuil re Sgeul
Air an Fhein nach fhachd thu riamh.

CLERICH. 2.
Air ma chumhas amhic Fhein
Ga bein leal bhi leachd air Fhein
Fuaim nan Sailm air feadh mo bhioil *
Gur he sud be Cheoil damh Fhein.

OSSHIAN. 3.
Na bi lu Coimheadadh do Shailm
Re fianichd Erin nan Arm nochd
A Clerich gur lan olc leum
Nach sgarain do Chean red Chorp.

CLERICH. 4.
Sin faoil Chomrich sa Fhir mhoir
Laoidh do Bheoil gur binn leum Fhein
Tagamid suas Altair Fhein
Bu bhinn liom bhi leachd air Fhein.

OSSHIAN. 5.
Nam bidhin thu Clerich Chaoimh
Air an Traidh ha Siar fa dheas
Aig Eass libridh na'n Shruth sheamh
Air an Fhein bu Mhor do Mheas.

OSSIAN AND THE CLERK.

OSSHIAN. 1.
O Clerk that singest the Psalms ! I think thy notions are rude ; that thou wilt not hear my songs, of the heroes of Fingal (*Fhein*), whom thou hast never seen.

CLERK. 2.
I find thy greatest delight is in relating the stories of the actions of Fingal and his heroes; but the sound of the Psalms is sweeter between my lips than the songs of Fingal.

OSSHIAN. 3.
If thou darest to compare thy Psalms to the old heroes of Ireland (*Erin*)† with their drawn weapons, Clerk ! I am much of opinion, I should be sorely vexed if I did not sever thy head from thy body.

CLERK. 4.
That is in thy mercy, great Sir ! the expressions of thy lips are very sweet to me. Let us rear the altar of Fingal ; ‡ I would think it sweet to hear of the heroes of Fingal.

OSSHIAN. 5.
If, my beloved Clerk ! thou wert at the South West shore, by the fall of Lever, of the slow-rolling stream, thou wouldest highly esteem the heroes of Fingal.

* Mr. Mac-Arthur, minister in Mull, declared to me that he could remember having heard the following poem of *Ossian agus an Clerich*, as long as he could remember any thing.

† Here Fingal and his heroes seem to be expressly attributed to Ireland. Fingal is distinguished as Irish also, in v. 8.

‡ Ossian and St. Patrick are ever represented as disputing, whether the Christian religion or the stories of Fhein were to be preferred. Here St. Patrick appears willing to acknowledge the superiority of the latter ; and to rear an altar, not to God, but Fingal.

6.
Bean neachd air Anam an Laoich
Bu ghairbhe Fraoich ansgach greish
Fean Mac-Cumhail Cean nan Sloigh
O san air a leainte'n Teass.

7.
La dhuine fiaghach na'n Dearg
'S nach derich an Tealg nar Cat
Gu facas deich mile Barc
Air Traidh a teachd air Lear.

8.
Shesaabh sin rul ail an Leirg
Thionnail an Fhein as gach Taoibh
Seachd Catha—urcharu gu prop
Gur e dhiahd mu Mhachd Nin Taoig.

9.
Shanig an Cabhlach gu Tir
Greadhin nach bu bhin hair leinn
Bu lionar ann Pubul Sroil
Ga thoigbhail leoos an eean.

10.
Hog iad an Coishri on Choill
Schuir iad orra an Airm ghaidh
San air Gualin gach Fhir mhor
Is thog siad orra on Traidh.

11.
Labhair Mac Cumhail ri Fhein
An fhidir shibh fein co na Sloigh
Nan nd fis ruigh shibh co Bhuidhin-bhorb
Bheir an Deanncal cruaidh san strachd.

12.
Sin nuair huirt Connan aris
Co bail leal a Ricogh bhi ann ?
Coshaoleadh tu Fhinn nan Cath
Bhiodh ann ach Flath na Riogh.

13.
Co gheomeid an air Fhein
Rechidh a ghabhail Sgeul don Ishuadh
'Sa bheridh hugain e gun Chleth
Sgum beireadh ee Breith is Buaidh.

14.
Sin nuair huirt Connan aris
Co bail leal a Riogh dhul ann
Ach Feargheas fior-ghlic do Mhachd
O she chleachd bhi dul nan Ceann ?

15.
Beir a Mhallachd a Connain Mhaoil
Huirt an Feargheas bu chaoin Cruth
Rachansa ghabhail an Sgeil
Don Fhein 'scho bann air do Ghuth.

16.
Ghluais an Feargheas armoil og
Air an Rod an Coinneamh nan'm fhear
'Sdehfisrich e le Comhradh foil
Co na Sloigh sho higair Lear ?

6.
My blessing attend the soul of that hero, whose fury was violent in battle; Fingal, son of Comhal, chief of the host! who gained great renown from that contest.

7.
One day that we were at the chace, looking for red-deer, not being successful in meeting with our game, we saw the rowing of ten thousand barks, coming along the surface of the sea, towards our shore.

8.
We all stood on the side of a hill; the followers of Fingal assembled from every quarter; seven tribes surrounded the son of Teague's (*Taoig*) daughter.

9.
The fleet came to shore, and there appeared a great multitude that seemed not disposed to friendship; and there was many a tent of silk raised over them.

10.
They bore away from the woods; they put on their beautiful armour on every great man's shoulder; and they bore away from the shore.

11.
The son of Comhal spoke to his heroes, " Can ye know who is this cruel people ? or do ye know who is the author of the furious battle on this shore ?"

12.
Then said Connan again, " Whom, O King, dost thou suppose them to be? or who shouldest thou think it should be? O thou Fingal of battles ! but the flower of Kings ?" (*Manos King of Norway*).

FINGAL. 13.
" Who shall we find among our heroes, that will go to get word of the people, and will bring us good intelligence, he shall have my applause and favour ?"

14.
Then says Connan again, " Whom, O King, would you chuse to go, but your very wise son Fergus ? since he is used to go on this business."

15.
" My curse on thee, bare-headed Connan," says Fergus of the fair complexions : " I will go and enquire about the heroes, but not for thy sake."

16.
Young warlike Fergus went away to the road to meet the men. He enquired with a mild voice, " Who were the multitude that came over the sea ?"

17.

Manus fuileach fearich fiar
Mac Riogh Beatha nan Sgia Dearg.
Ard Riogh Lochlin Ceann nan Clear.
Giolla bo Mhor Fiabh as Fearg.

18.

Ciod a ghluaise Bhuin borb
O Rioghachd Lochlan nan Colg scann
Mar han a Mheadacha air Fhion
A hanig air Triath hair Lear.

19.

Air do Laimsa Fheargheas fhoile,
Asan Fhein ga Mor do shuim
Cha gabh fin Cumha gan B'hran,
Agus a Bhean a hoirl o Fhean.

20.

Bheiridh an Fhein Combrag cruaidh
Dod Shluadh nia'm fuighe tu Bran,
Is bheridh Fean Combrag trein
Dhuil fein mum fuighe tu Bhean.

21.

Hanig Feargheas mo Bhrair fein.
'Sbu Chosbhail ri Grein a Chruth
'Shisidh e Sgeile go foil
Ga' bosgaradh mor a Gehuth.

22.

Mac Riogh Lochlan sud faoin Traibh
Go de'n fa gho bhi ga Chleth?
Cha gabh e gun Chomhrag dlu
Na do Bhean's do Chu faoi bhreth.

23.

Chaoidh cha tugainse mo Bhean
Dodh 'aon Neach ata fuidh 'n Ghrein
'Scha mho mheir mi Bran gu brach
Gus an leid am Bas na Bheil.

24.

Labhair Mac Cumhaii ri Goll
Smor an Glonn duin bi nar tosd
Nach tugamid Comhrag borb
Do Riogh Lochlan nan Sciadh breachd.

25.

Seachd Altramain Lochain lain
Se labhair Goll gun fhas Cheilg
Sair libhse gur Moran Sluaidh
Bheir mi'm brigh fa'm buaidh gu leir.

17.

Bloody Magnus of the manly form, son of
King Beatha of the red shield; chief King
of Lochlin (*Norway*), and head of men, a
man of furious appearance.

18.

"What moved thee, thou fierce man! from
the kingdom of Lochlin with fierce appearance; if it was not to increase our warriors,
that the hero came over the sea?"

19.

"By thy hand, thou mild Fergus! tho'
thou art great among the heroes, we will
not take a reward without Bran, and we
will take the wife of Fingal himself."

FERGUS.   20.

"Our heroes will give thy people hard
battle, before thou shalt get Bran; and
Fingal will himself fight thee hard, before
thou shalt get his wife."

21.

My brother Fergus came with his com-
plexion like the sun; to tell the tale mildly,
though his voice was loud.

22.

"The son of the king of Lochlin is on the
shore: Why should I conceal it? He will
not depart without hard battle, or thy wife
and thy dog as a reward."

FINGAL.   23.

"I never will give my wife to any one under the sun: neither will I give Bran for
ever, till death takes hold of my mouth."

24.

Comhal's son spoke to Gaul, "It is great
shame for us to be quiet; that we do not
give hard battle to the King of Lochlin, of
the spotted shield." *

25.

"The seven brave sons, of the little lake
of Lano, says Gaul without guile; you,
think them a great multitude, but I will
conquer them." †

---

* Neither Mac-Nab, nor any other Highlander, to whom I shewed this poem, ever
seemed to conceive, that there was any affinity between it and the Ossian of Mr. Macpherson: but, on comparing it with the poem called Fingal, I find the following
parallel passages, book IV. some parts of which are a translation of the above song, though
quite on a different subject. 24. "Behold," said the King of generous shields, "how
Lochlin divides on Lena—Let every chief among the friends of Fingal take a dark troop
of those that have grown so high. Nor let a son of the echoing groves bound on the
waves of Inistore."

† "Mine, said Gaul, be the seven chiefs, that came from Lano's Lake."

26.   Prios
Se huirt an Tosgar bu mhor Brigh
Diongamsa Riogh Insc-Tore
S Cinn a Dha chomhirlich dheig
Leig faoi 'm choimhir fein an Coisg.

27.
Iarla Muthuin smor a Ghlonn
Se huirt Diarmaid donn gun ghuin
Coisge mise sud dar Fein
No tcuitim fein air a shon.

28.
Gur he dhabh mi fein fos Laimh
Gad ha mi gun Chail an Nochd
Riogh Termiu na'n Comhrag teann,
'Sgo sgarrain a Chean re Chorp.

29.
Beubh Beanneachd's buinibh buaidh
Huirt Mac Cumhail nan Gruaidh dearg
Manus Mac Gharra nan Sloidh
Diongaidh mise ga mor Fhearg.

30.
Noiche sin duinne gu Lo
Bainmaig lein abhi gun Cheoil
Fleagh gu fairsing fion is Ceir
Se bheidh aig an Fhein ga ol.

31.
Chuncas mu'n do scar an Lo
A gabhail Doigh an sa Ghuirt
Meirg Riogh Lochlan an aigh
Ga hogail on Traibh nan Nuchd.

32.
Chuir shinn Deo-ghreine ri Crann
Brattaeh Fhein bu gharga Trus'h
Lom-lan do Cloc'haibh oir
Aguinue bu mhorra Meas.

33.
Jommaid Cloimh Dorn-chan oir
Jommaid Sroil ga chuir ri Crann
'N Cath Mhic Cumhail Fean nan fleadh
'Sbo Lionfar Sleadh osair Ceann.

26.
Then says Oscar of mighty strength, "Give to me the King of Inistore (*the island of Wild Boars*); his twelve nobles have a sweet voice, leave me to quell them." *

27.
"Earl Mudan's glory is great," says brown Dermid without malice ; " I will quell him for thy heroes, or fall in the attempt." †

28.
I myself took in hand, tho' I am at this night without vigour, King Terman of the close battles, that I should sever his head from his body. ‡

29.
" Deserve blessings, and gain the victory," says Comhal's son with the red cheeks : "Magnus son of Gharra of multitudes, I will conquer, though great is his fury in battle." §

30.
From night to day, we seldom wanted music : a wide house, wine, and wax, are what we used to have, when we drank.

31.
We saw, before the dawn of day, the iron King of Lochlin, taking possession of the field ; coming in his youth, from the shore, before the men. ǁ

32.
We set up decently to a standard the colours of fierce Fingal : they were full of golden stones, and with us much esteemed. ¶

33.
Many a gold-hilted sword, many a flag was raised to its staff ; in the hospitable son of Comhal's battle : and many a javelin was above us. **

* Let Inistore's dark King, said Oscar, come to the sword of Ossian's son : To mine the King of Iniscon, said Connal heart of steel.

† Or Mudan's Chief, or I, said brown-haired Dermid, shall sleep on clay-cold earth.

‡ My choice, though now so weak and dark, was Terman's battling King. I promised with my hand, to win the hero's dark brown shield.

§ Blest and victorious be my chiefs, said Fingal of the mildest look ; Swaran, King of roaring waves, thou art the choice of Fingal !"—The blessings here are evidently Christian ; Macpherson, in his translation, has very happily given them a different air— The next verse in the poem above is evidently corrupt, and improper.

ǁ This verse, though following the challenges of the Fingalians, in my copy, is evidently analogous to Fingal's speech at the beginning of them in Macpherson.

¶ This verse, like the former, is transposed. In Macpherson it precedes verse 31. "We reared the sun-beam of battle, the standard of the king : each hero exulted with joy, as waving it flew on the wind. It was studded with gold above, as the blue wide shell, of the nightly sky." The word translated by Mr. M. Sun-beam, *Deo-ghreine*, was by Mr. Darrach interpreted, Colours ; as being more intelligible in English, though less literal.

** "Each hero," adds Macpherson, "had his standard too, and each his gloomy men.'

34.

Jommaid cotan, jommaid Triach
Jommaid scia as lurich dharamh
Jommaid Draoisich's mac Riogh
'Scha raibb fear riamh dheu gun arm.

34.

Many a coat of mail, many a hero, many a
shield, many a great breast-plate, many a
king's son ; and there was none of them
without a weapon.

35.

Jommaid Cloigid maisich cruaidh
Jommaid Tuath is Jommaid Gath
'N Cath Riogh Lochlin na'm pios
Bu lionfar Mac Riogh is Flath.

35.

Many a handsome steel helmet, many a
battle-ax (the Lochabar Ax, see Gal. Ant. p.
261.), many a dart, in the host of arms of
the King of Lochlin of shells ; and many
heroes, the sons of kings.

36.

Rinneadir an 'Nuirnig chruaigh
'S bhrisseadear air Buaidh na'n Gall
Chrom shinn ar Cean an sa Chath
Is rein gach Flath mar a Ghcall.

36.

They prayed fervently, and the forces of
the strangers were broken : we bowed our
heads in the battle, and every hero did as
he had promised.*

37.

Hachair Mac Cumhail na'n Cuach
Agus Manus na'n ruag gun Adh ·
Ri cheil 'ann an Tuitim an tslaaidh
Chlerich nach bo cruaidh au Cas.

37.

The son of Comhal of the drinking horns,
and Magnus the unfortunate, met together
in the middle of the multitude : Clerk, was
not that a dreadful case ?

38.

Go'm be sud an Turleum tean
Mar Dheanna a bheridh da Ord
Cath fuilich an da Riogh
Go'm bo ghuinneach briogh an Colg.

38.

Was not that a close fight, like the strokes
of two hammers, the bloody battle of the
two kings, whose countenances were very
furious ? †

39.

Air brisseadh do Sge an Dearg
Air eridh dhoibh Fearg is Fraoch
Heilg iad am Buil air an lar
'S hug iad Spairn an da Laoich.

39.

After the red shield (Sge Dearg) was broken,
their countenances being fierce ; they threw
their weapons to the ground, and the two
heroes wrestled for the victory.‡

40.

Cath fuileach an da Riogh
San leinne bu chian an Closs
Bha Clachan agus Talamh trom
Amosgladh faoi Bhonn an Coss.

40.

The bloody battle of the two kings ; we
longed for their separation : there were
stones and heavy earth, opening below the
soles of their feet.§

41.

Leagur Riogh Lochlan gan Adh
Am fianish Chaich air an Raoch
'Sair san gad nach bhon air Riogh
Chuiridh ceangeal nan bu Chaoil.

41.

The unfortunate King of Lochlin was over-
thrown, in presence of the rest, among the
heath ; and, though it did not become a
king, his feet and hands were tied. ‖

---

* This verse is not only Christian, but even superstitious : in Macpherson it is expressed somewhat differently : " The gloomy ranks of Lochlin fell, like the banks of the
roaring Cona : " our arms were victorious on Lena, each chief fulfilled his promise."

† The following verses are as analogous to the battle of Fingal and Swaran, Fingal,
B. V. as the verses foregoing to the passages above quoted, from Macpherson : " When
the two heroes met, there was the clang of arms ! There every blow, like the hundred
hammers of the furnace : Terrible is the battle of the kings ; dreadful the look of their eyes."

‡ " Their dark brown shields (Sge Dearg) are cleft in twain. Their steel flies broken
from their helms. They fling their weapons down. Each rushes to his hero's grasp.
Their sinewy arms bend round each other : they turn from side to side ; and strain,
and stretch, their large and spreading limbs below."

§ " But when the pride of their strength arose, they shook the hill with their heels.
Rocks tumble from their places on high : the green-headed bushes are overturned."

‖ At length the strength of Swaran fell : the King of the Groves is bound.

42.

Sin nuair huirt Connan Maoil
Mac Mornadh bha riabh ri Hòle,
Cumur ruim Manus nan lan
'Sgo sgarrain an Ceann re Chorp.

43.

Cha neil agam Cairdeas na Gaoil
Riutsa Connain Mhaoil gun Fhoalt
O'n harla mi'n Grasan Fhein
'Sansa lcum na bi faoi fu'd Smachd.

44.

O harla thu'm Grasabd fein
Cha'n iommair mi Bend Flath
Fuasglath mi husa o'm Fhein
A Laimh Threun gu cur mor Chath.

45.

'Sgeibh thu do raoghin aris
Nuairaheid thu do'd Thir fein
Cairdeas is commun doghna
Na do Lamh achuir faoi'm Fhein.

46.

Cha chuir mi mo Laimh faoi'd Fhein
Ncian a Mhairtheas Cail am Chorp
Aon Bhuille Taoighe Fhein
Saithreach deinn no rcinncas ort.

47.

Mi fein agus Mathair is Goll
Triur bo mho Glonn san Fhein
Ged na sinn gun Draofich no Colg
Ach easteachd ri Hord Clcir.

42.

Then says bald-headed Connan, son of Mornah, who was always drinking, "Hold, Magnus of the swords, whilst I sever his head from his body."

MAGNUS. 43.

"I have no friendship nor love for thee, bald Connan without hair : but though I am in Fingal's mercy, I would rather be so, than under thy authority."

FINGAL. 44.

"Since thou art in Fingal's mercy, I will allow no harm to thee : I will set thee at liberty from amongst my heroes ; thou strong hand to fight the battles !"

45.

"And thou shalt get thy own choice again, when thou shalt return to thy own country : friendship and unity always, or else to be revenged, of our heroes." *

MAGNUS. 46.

"I will not take revenge of your heroes, as long as there is breath in my body ; nor will I strike one stroke against thyself. I repeat what I have done to you." †

47.

Myself, my Father, and Gaul, were the three who had most children, amongst our heroes ; though we are now without strength, hearkening to clergymen's orders.

Many curious remarks might be made on the language of the foregoing poem, which abounds with words derived from the Latin, Danish, and Saxon tongues ; as Clerich, Chorp, Fhir, Nochd, from the former ; Barc, Iarla, Cotan, Brisseadh, from the latter : many particularities also worthy our attention occur in the style and versification ; such are the paucity of epithets, the love of alliteration (see verse 29, l. 1.), and the frequent repetition of lines in every respect the same, as in Homer, probably with a design to assist the memory (as verse 3, l. 4, v. 28, l. 4, and 42, l. 4,— v. 14, l. 1, v. 42, l. 1, &c.) ; but because it would infringe too much on your Magazine to enlarge upon these subjects, I shall leave them to the acuteness of your readers.

* In the sixth book of Fingal, this passage also is found : "Raise to-morrow," says Fingal to Swaran, "raise thy white sails to the wind, thou brother of Agandecca.—— Or dost thou chuse the fight ? The combat, which thy fathers gave to Trenmor, is thine ! that thou mayest depart renowned, like the Sun setting in the West !"

† "King of the Race of Morven," said the Chief of resounding Lochlin, "never will Swaran fight with thee, first of a thousand heroes !" I found these parallel passages, on a slight comparison of the above poem with Macpherson ; perhaps a stricter search might find out many more. This poem under the title of Manos, has been likewise published by Mr. Smith, Gal. Ant. Edinb. 1780, p. 250 ; but the parallel passages, in his copy and mine, are scarcely so numerous as those above quoted from Macpherson : our copies agree only in the 16th, 21st, 22nd, 35th, 39th, 41st, 42nd, 43rd, and 44th verses of the above poem. Even the story of the two copies is not the same : in Smith, besides many other differences, the poem concludes with the death of Manos ; in my copy, Manos is only bound, like Swaran in Macpherson.

Shaw, the last antagonist of Ossian, observes, that he could not meet with any songs, in the Highlands, which mentioned Swaran King of Lochlin: but that they all spoke of Manos or Magnus a name of later times. Perhaps the foregoing might be one of the songs he met with.

The two following poems I received from Mac-Nab, at the same time with the last. The first of them relates to the Death of Dermid: the History of a Song, on which subject I have already sent you, on the authority of Mr. Stuart of Blair.* The differences, which appear between the following song, and that described by Mr. Stuart, are not very great; and they serve mutually to explain one another. I there observed, that another song on this subject, much longer, and containing a greater number of circumstances, had been inserted by Mr. Smith, in his Galic Antiquities.† Mr. Smith's poem opening with an address to Cona, and Mount Golbun; describes Fingal's going out to hunt on the latter, and relates, that Dermid hearing the cry of the dogs, left the embraces of his wife, to join the chace. She following him, meets with an old man, mourning over his own wife and son; the latter of whom, having fallen at the chace, through the loss of his spear, she determined to pursue her husband, with a supernumerary one. Dermid joins Fingal, and engages the boar, incited by the promised rewards of that monarch. He loses his spear, but receives another from his wife; who is slain herself, by a wandering arrow. With the second spear, he pierces the breast of the boar; but the shaft being broken, he draws his sword, and kills the animal. Connan, the Thersites of the Highland songs, who had been Dermid's rival in love, then dares him to measure the boar; which he does, first in the same direction with the bristles, and receives no injury: but, being farther provoked by Connan, measures him again the contrary way, and the bristles piercing his feet he is slain.‡ His wife, not yet expired, mourns over him; and then dies. Their interment is described, and the poem concludes with Ossian's funeral song. Such is the history of Smith's poem, which in some respects coincides with the following, and in many differs from it: what few parallel passages there are I shall insert in the notes. Mr. Darrach, the translator of the former, was so kind as to translate these also for me.

MAR MHARB DIARMID AN TORC NIMHE.	HOW DERMID KILLED THE POISONOUS WILD BOAR.
EISDIBH beag ma's ail leibh Laoidh Air chuideachd a chaoidh so chuaidh Air Beinn Ghuilbenn's air Fuinn fial 'S air mac o Duine nan Sgeul truagh: Dh'imis iad a bu mhor an fheall Air mac o Duine bu dearg beul Diol do bhein Ghuilben a shealg. Tuirc, nach feadh airm a chaoidh Dh'eirich a bheist as a suain	GIVE ear for a little, if you are fond of a poetical account, of those people that are now dead; and that went to Mount Golbun: and likewise of hospitable Fingal, and the Son of O Duine of the Mournful Tales. They prevailed, with great treachery, on the Son of O Duine of the Red Lip, to go to Mount Golbun, to hunt a wild boar, that no weapon could subdue. The beast

* See p. 5.
† Gal. Ant. p. 187 to 202.
‡ The mode of mensuration here meant was performed by putting the feet one before the other along the boar's back, according to the original mode of measuring by the FOOT.

Dh'amhairc i uaip an gleann
Dh'fhairich i faragra nam Fian
Teachd a noir 's a niar na Ceann.
Mac o Duine nach d' ob diamh
Chuir e'n t sleagh an dail an Tuirc
Bhris e'innt 'an crann mu thri
Bu reachdar leis a bhi sa mhuic
Tharruing e shean lann o'n Truaill
Bhuigneadh buaidh anns gach blar
Mharbh mac o Duine a bheist
Thachair dha feir a bhi slan
'Shuidh sinn uil air aon Chnoc
Luidh mor sprochd air Ceann flath Fail
Air bhi dha fada na thosd
Labhair e's gum b'ole a chial
"Tomhais a Dhiarmaid f'a fochd
Cia mead troigh 's an Torc a Niar
"Seath troighe deug de fhior thomhas
Tha'm frioghan na Muice fiadhaich
Cho'n e fin iddir a tomha's
Tomhais a ris i Dhiarmaid
Tomhais a Dhiarmid a ris
Na aghaidh gu min an Torc
'S leatsa do roghair ga chionn
Tuil 'igh nan arm rann-gheur goirt.
    Dh'eirich e sb'en turas gaidh
Thomhais e dhoibh an Torc
Tholl am friogh bha nimheil garg
Bonn an Laoich bu gharbh san trod
"Aon deoch dhamhs' ad Chuaich Fhinn
Fhir nam briathra blatha binn
Fon chaill mi mo bhrigh 'smo bhlaogh
O choin, gur truagh mur tabhair
"Cho toir mise dhuit mo Chuach
'Scha mho chabhras mi ar t iota
O's beag a rinn thes dom' leas
'Sgur mor a rinn thu do m'aimhleas
"Cha d'rinn mise cron ort riamh
Thall na bhos, a noir na niar
Ach iunichd 'le Grain am braidd
Sa huir gam thobhairt fa gheassaibh.

awakened out of his sound sleep, he looked about him round the glen, and perceived the noise of the heroes, (*Fian*) coming east and west about him. The Son of O Duine, who never shunned a warlike enterprise, aimed his javelin at the boar; broke the shaft thereof in three pieces, and was displeased to find it so in the boar. He drew from the scabbard his trusty blade, that obtained victory in battle: the Son of O Duine killed the beast, and he himself was safe.* We all sat upon one hill, at which time Fingal was seized with a deep melancholy: after a long silence, he spoke in a fierce manner: "Dermid! measure the boar, how many feet he measures to the westward!"—"Sixteen feet of neat measure, the bristles of the wild boar measure!" (*Fingal*) "That is not all the measure; measure it again, Dermid, measure it, Dermid, again, against the bristles, for so doing, you shall have your choice of my warlike weapons."†

He got up and undertook the hard task: he measured the boar to them. The venomous coarse bristles pierced the soles of the hero's feet, and severe was the enterprize. "One drink out of Fingal's cup (*Chuach Fhinn*). You with the warm sweet words! Since I have lost my strength and vigour in this attempt, it is cruel if you deny me." —"I will not give you my cup (*Chuach*), nor will I quench your drought; as you have done little to please me, and have done much to offend me."—"I never did you any harm, up or down, east or west; but proceeded rashly to recover myself of my metamorphoses."‡

---

* Smith (p. 194.) gives this passage as follows: "With all his terrible might the chief lifts his spear; like a meteor of death red issuing from Lano's cloud, a flood of light, it quick descends. The head is lodged in the rough breast of the boar: the shaft flies over trees, through air. His sword is in the hero's hand, the old companion of his deeds in the hour of danger. Its cold point pierces the heart of the foe. The boar, with all his blood and foam, is stretched on earth." Smith adds, that the Clan of Campbell, said to be descended from Dermid, assume the boar's head for their crest from this event. Smith calls Dermid the son of Duino, p. 198; Macpherson calls him the son of Duthno. Fingal, B.V.

† Smith (p. 194.) alters this passage a little; and ascribes it to Connan, in the room of Fingal, as I have already said. "Measure, said Connan, that little soul, the boar which thou hast slain! Measure him with thy foot bare, a larger hath not been seen!" The foot of Dermid slides softly along the grain, no harm hath the hero suffered. "Measure, said Connan, the boar against the grain! and thine, chief of spears, shall be the boon thou wilt ask." The soul of Dermid was a stranger to fear; he obeyed again the voice of Connan. But the bristly back of Golbun's boar, sharp as his arrows, and strong as his spear, pierces with a thousand wounds his feet.—Dermid falls, like a tall pine on the heath." A boar sixteen feet long is large indeed!

‡ Smith omits this conversation: he thus speaks of it in a note, p. 195; "Such as may here miss the dialogue, concerning *Chuach Fhinn*, or the medicinal cup of Fingal,

Gleann sith an gleann fiar rar taubh
'Slion 'ar guth Feidh ann, 's loin,
Gleann an tric an raibh an Fhiann
A Nor 's an iar an deigh nan Con
An Gleann sin fos Beinn Ghuilbin ghuirm
'S ailidh tulachan tha fo'n Ghrein
'Stric a bha na struthain dearg
'N deigh do'n Fhian bhi seal an fheidh.
Sin e na shine air an Raon
Mac O Duin' air a thaobh feall
Na shine re laobh an Tuirc
Sin sgeul th'agair duit gu dearbh.
Guill ei deadh oir is eab
'S an cigin nan Creach nach ganu
Lamh bu mhor Gaisg is griomh
O choin mar tsia'n faoidh sa ghleann.

The glen alongside of us is dark ; numerous
there are the ruttings of deer, and the
voices of blackbirds : in that glen, the
heroes often went east and west, after their
dogs : the glen under verdant Mount
Golbun, whose hillocks are the fairest
beneath the sun : where often the rivulets
ran red, after the heroes had killed their
deer. There, extended on the green, lies
the son of O Duine, stretched on his lovely
side along the boar, and clad in all his
armour. This tale of truth have we to tell.
Alas ! Great is our loss ! The hand that
performed many valiant deeds ! the chief
of warriors lies in the glen !

In the foregoing Poem it deserves to be remarked, that Fingal is not
only treated with little reverence, according to a former observation of
mine, * but is even represented as guilty of treachery. Mr. Stuart's
Narration of the Death of Dermid agrees with the Poem above in this
respect; whereas Mr. Smith has chosen to represent it differently : and
more agreeably with the uncontaminated honour of Fingal, in the rest of
his publication, and in the Ossian of Macpherson. Smith also attempts,
in a note, p. 194, to palliate and cover the superstitious notion of the fatal
consequences produced, by walking along the back of a boar, in a direction
contrary to the bristles : no doubt, because he would have us suppose,
that the natives of the Highlands, unlike all other nations, have been ever
guided by truth and reason. I wish the same intention had not hid many
similar notions from the public : for it is among such traditional prejudices,
that we must look for national character, and the true knowledge of
mankind. Reason is ever the same, but folly various. They would also,
at the same time, have stamped greater authenticity on the Poems which
should have contained them.

I am inclined to suspect, that there are in the foregoing Song some
words directly derived from the English, as Bheist, thri, &c.

The next Poem, is an account of the death of Bran, Fingal's celebrated
dog : which has not, so far as I know, been ever published before. It does
not seem very clear what sort of dog he was, though the Poem concludes
with a singular description of him ; wherein also is contained a curious
enumeration of the peculiar marks of excellence in dogs.

MUR MHARBHADH BRAN.

LAG is lag orin ars' a chorr
'S fada ona mo luirg 'am dheigh
Nam brisins 'i a nochd
Cail am faighin lus na leigh.

HOW BRAN WAS KILLED.

"WE are failed ! we are failed !" says the
heron, "my shank bone is long behind ;
should I break it in the night, where could
I find a physician, or medicine ?"

will remember, that it is of so different a complection from the rest of the poem, that no
apology needs be made for rejecting it, as the interpolation of some later bard." Smith
probably found it not easily susceptible of ornament ; and inconsistent with his plan, as
throwing the blame on Fingal ; which were certainly sufficient reasons for his omitting
it. I am not adequately acquainted with the secret history of Dermid, to explain what
is meant by his metamorphoses, in my copy.

* See p. 5.

Leighisins 'i ars an dreolan
O'n leighis mi moran rombad
A chorribh tha o's ma cheann
'S mis a leighis Fionn nam sleagh
An lamhaobh sinn an torc liath
'S iomad Fian a bha san t sleibh
'S iomad culean taobh-gheal seang
Bha taobh ri taobh sa bheinn bhuig.
'Nuair shuidhich Fionn an t sealg
'Sin nuair ghabh Bran fearg ra chuid.
Throidd an da choin anns an t sliahh
Bran gu dian agus cu Ghuill
Mu'n d'fheadas smachd a chuir ais Bran
Dhealaich e naoi uilt ra dhruim
Dh'eirich Goll mor mac Smail
Cuis nach bu choir mu cheann coin
Bhagair e an lamh an roibh Bran
Gun-dail thoirt da ach a mharbhadh.
Dh'eirich Ossian beag mac Fhinn
'S cuig cead deug an codhail Ghuill
Lanhair i an cora ard
Caisgim do luath garg a Ghuill
Bhuail mibuille do'n eil bhuigh
'S do na bailgibh fuin diarneach
Dh'adh 'laigh mi an t'or na cheann
'S truagh a rinn mi 'm beud ra theinn
Sheall mo chuilean thara ghualain
B'iognadh leis mi ga bhualadh
Ar lamh fin leis 'n do bhuaileadh Bran
'S truagh on ghualain nach do sgar
Mun d'rinn mi am beud a bhos
Gur truagh nach ann eug a chuaidheas.
    Ciod a bhuaidh a bhiodhair Bran
Arsa Connan nabhreach miar ?
    Fon a b'aois cuilean do Bhran
'S son chuir mi conn-ial air
Chan fhacas am fianibh fail
Lorg feidh an deigh fhagail
Bu mhaith e hun an dorain duinn
Bu mhaith e thairt eisg a h abhainn
Gum b'fhearr Bran a mharbha bhroc
Na coin an tal on' d'thainig
A cheud leige fhuair Bran riamh
Air druim na coille coir liath
Namar do gach fiadh ar bith
Mharbh Bran air a cheud rith.
    Cassa buidhe bha aig Bran
Da lios dhutha as torr geal
Druim uaine on suidh an sealg
Cluase corrach cro'-dhearg.§

"I would cure thee," says the wren, "as I cured many before thee : O heron, that lookest down upon me ! It was I who cured the blythe Fingal, the day the grey boar was slain." Many a hero was then upon the moor ; many a handsome white-sided greyhound, stood side by side, on the yellow mountain. When Fingal prepared for hunting, Bran grew angry about his food. Then the two dogs fought upon the moor, fierce Bran and Gaul's dog. Before Bran could be managed, he severed nine joints from the other's back. The great Gaul, the son of Smail,* arose, incensed at the loss of his dog ; he threatened to put the hand that held Bran to immediate death. Little Ossian, the son of Fingal, got up, and fifteen hundred more,+ to meet Gaul and spoke with a loud voice.

"Let me stop thy bold hand, Gaul ! I struck Bran with the yellow thong, and sore did I repent : at which the famous Bran looked over his shoulder, surprised at my striking him. Pity it was, the hand that struck Bran had not been first severed from the shoulder.—Ere I committed the deed, I could wish I had been no more." ‡

"What were the qualifications of Bran ?" says rash Connan—(Ossian). "Since Bran was a whelp, and since I got a collar upon him, neither Fingal nor his heroes ever saw the track of a deer that left him. He was excellent at the otter; was good at taking fish out of the water ; and was more famous at killing badgers than any dog of his time. The first chace that ever Bran went, above the wood of Cori-liath, nine of all kinds of deer Bran ran down in the first pursuit."

"Bran's feet were of a yellow hue ; both his sides black, and his belly white ; his back was of an eel-colour, famous for the sport ; his ears sharp, erect, and of a scarlet colour."

I have deferred sending you the following poems, in the hope that I should have been able to accompany them with a translation ; for which

---

* This Gaul, the son of Smail, is surely a different person from Gaul, the son of Morni, of Macpherson and Smith—but such varieties are common in the Highland songs.
    † These huntings seem to have been undertaken by the whole clan together.
    ‡ Bran appears to have been slain by this blow. *The yellow thong* seems to have had some peculiarly fatal power in it, by this account of its effects.
    § In the first stanza of this poem, l. 1 *for* orin r. oirn ; l. 2 *for* ona r. cna ; l. 6 *for* rombad r. romhad.

purpose, Dr. Willan, of Bartlet's Buildings, Holborn, was so kind as to transmit them to a friend of his in Scotland. But the translation not having found its way to London, after a much longer delay than I had reason to expect, you now receive them in their original Erse. Should I hereafter receive this translation, I shall certainly trouble you with it. In the meanwhile, if any of your numerous readers, who understand Erse, will oblige me, and, I trust, the public, by rendering this translation unnecessary, I have no doubt you will think yourself happy to insert it.

It becomes me to make some apology for the numerous errors in orthography, which must necessarily have found their way into these Erse poems; published as they are by a stranger to the language. I can only say, that it has been my constant endeavour to be as correct as possible; though I am conscious, that nothing is more easy than to mistake one letter for another in an unknown tongue. There is, however, this consideration to be made, which perhaps will excuse many apparent errors: that the writers of Erse, in the Scottish Highlands, by no means agree in their mode of spelling. The reading and writing of the Scottish Erse has made hitherto but a small progress; it certainly never appeared in the form of printing till of late years. What manuscripts there were, seem to have been known to few; and even those few were, perhaps, obliged to Ireland for their knowledge.* Every one, to whom I showed these poems in the Highlands for translation, told me, that they were written in the Irish dialect; and indeed they evidently appear to attribute Fingal to Ireland.†

I received the two following poems from Mac-Nab, at the same time with those which have preceded them.

DUAN A MHUILEARTICH.

La do'n Fhein air Tullich toir
Re abhrac Erin onan tiomichil
Chunaire iad air Bharibh Thonn
An Tarrachd eitidh aitail crom
She bainm do'n Dfhuadh nach ro fann
      maunlich
Am Muilleartich maoil ruaigh mathnn
Bha Haodin du-ghlas air dhreich guail
Bha Deid carbadich claoin ruaigh
Bha aoin Suil ghloggich na Ceann
'Sbu luaigh i na Ruinich Maoirinn
Bha greann ghlas-duth air a Ceann
Mar dhroich Coill chrinich air chritheann
Ri abbarc nan Fian bu mhor Goil
      bhi
Tshauntich a Bhiast teachd nan Innis
Mhairbh i le Habbichd ciad Laoich
'So Gaira mor na Gairbh Chrnois
Cail a bheil Firr as fearr na Shud
An duigh an Fhein a Mhic Cubhail
Chuirinse shudair do Laibh
A Mhuileartich mhathion mahoil cham-
      mahaeh
Air Sca Luchd chumail nan Conn

Na bi oirne gad Mbaoithidh
Gheibh thu Cubhigh asgaibh Shith
Huirt Mac Cubhail an tard Riogh
Gad gheibhinse Brigh Erin rulle
A Hor 'sa Hairgid sa Huinbhis
Bear leom thu Chosgairt mo Tshleigh
Oscair Raoine sa Chaorrail
An Tshleigh shin ris a bheil thu fas
San aice ha do ghian-bhas
Caillidh tu dosa Chinn chrin
Re deo Mhac Ossian a dhearraigh
Bussa dhuit Ord Chrottidh nan Clach
A chaigne fud 'l Fhiaclan—
Na Cobhrig nan Fian fuillich
'N shin nar gherich fraoich na beist
Dherich Fiun flath na Feinigh
Dherich Oscur flath na fearr
Dherich Oscur agus Iullin
Dherich Ciar-dhuth Mao bramh
Dherich Goll Mor agus Connan
Dherich ne Laoich nac bo tiom
Laoich Mhic Cubhail nan Arm grinn
Agus rein iad Cro-coig-cath
Mun Arrichd eitidh san Gleann

A Cearthir Laoich abfhearr san fhein
Chobhrigidh i iad gu leir
Agus fhrithilidh Siad ma sheach
Mar ghath rinne na Lasrich
Hachir Mac Cubhail an Aigh
Agus a Bhiast Laibh air Laibh
Bha Druchd air Barribh a Lainne
Bha taibh a Cholla ri Guin bualidh
Bha Braoin ga Fhuil air na fraoichibh
Huil am Muileartich leis an Riogh
Ach Mathuil cha ban gun Strith
Deichin cha duair e mar Shin
O La Ceardich Loin Mhic Liobhain
Ghluais an Gothidh leis a Bhrigh
Gu Teich othar an Ard Riogh
'Sbu Sgeulidh le Gotha nan Cuan
     m' athion maoil ruagh
Gun do bharraigh am Muileartich
Mar dechidh ean Tailibh Tolc
Na mar do. bhathigh am Muir dhobhain
    Long
Caile àn rò Dhaoine air bith
Na bharraigh am Muileartich mathion

Cha ne bharbh i ach an Fhian
Buidhin leis nach gabhir Giabh
'S nach Deid Fua na Arrachdas
Fon Tshluaigh aluin Fhalt-bhui iommaidh
Bheir misc briathar a rist
Ma bharbhigh am Muileartich min
Nach fhag misc aoin na Ghleann
Tom Innis na Eilleain
Bheir mi breapadich air Muir
Agus Coragadich air Tir
    Crocoran
Agus ni mi Croran Coill
    Freibhichean
Ga tarruing hugam asa Taibhichean
'S mor an Luchd do Loingeas ban
Erin uille d Thogbhail
'S nach dechidh do Loingeas riabhair Sail
Na thoga Coigibh do dh' Erin
Mile agus Caogid Long
Sin Caibhlich an Riogh gu trom
A Dol gu Crichibh Erin
    fanagh
Air hi na Feinigh nan taragh.

CUBHA FHINN DO RIOGH LOCHLIN.

    ai
DEICH ciad Cuilean deich ciad Cu
Deich ciad Slaibhrigh air Mil chu
    Sleigh
Deich ciad Sealtuin chaoil Chatha
Deich ciad Brat min Datha
    Each
Deich ciad Gearaltich cruaigh Dearg
Deich ciad Nobul don Or dhearg
Deich ceud Maighdin le da Ghun
Deich ceid Mantul don Tshid Ur
Deich ceid Sonu a dherigh leat
Deich ciad Srian Oir & airgid.
    Riogh Lochlin.
Gad a gheibhidh Riogh Lochlin shud
'S na bha' Mhaoin 'sdo Tsheidin an Erin
Cha fhilligh e T'shluaigh air ais
Gus 'mbigh Erin rull' air Earras
    Suil gan dug Riogh Lochlin.
Uaigh chunnair e Brattich a tin
Amach & Gille gaiste air a Ceann
Air a lasc do Dh or Eirinich
Dibhuille Duibhne dualich
Ni shud Brattich Mhic Trein-bhuaghich.
    Dibhuille.
Cha ni shud ach an L ath luid neach
Brattich Dhiarmaid o Duibhne
'Snar bhigh an Fhian rull' amach
'Shi Liath-luidnich bu toisich
    Suil gan dug Riogh Lochlin, &c.

    Dibhuille.
Cha ni shud ach an Aoin Chasach ruaidh
Brattich Chaoilte nan Mor Tshluaidh
Brattach leis an sgoiltear Ciun
'S an doirtir Fuil gu Aoibranibh
    Suil, &c.
    Dibhuille.
Cha ni shud ach an Scuab ghabhigh
Brattach Oscur Chro' laidir
'Snar a ruigte Cath nan Cliar
Cha biach fhiarich ach Scuab-ghabuidh
    Suil, &c.
    Dibhuille.
Cha ni sud ach a Bhriachil bhreochil
Brattach Ghuill Mhoir Mhic Morni *
Nach dug 'Troigh air a hais
Gus n do chrith an Tailibh tromghlas
    Suil, &c. &c.
    Dibhuille.
'S misa dhuitsa na bheil ann
Ha Ghil ghreine an sud a tighin
As Naoigh Slaibhrinin aist a shios
    dail
Don Or bhuigh gun Dal Sgiabh
    i
Agus Naoigh nao lan-gheasgeach
Fo Cheann a huille Slaibhrigh
Atogairt air feo do Tshuaighthibh
Mar Cliabh-tragha gu Traigh
Bigh gair Chatha gad iummain.

* Here Gaul is called the son of Morni, see note * in p. 16 ; he is always called *Mhoir Ghuil*, or *Great Gaul*, and seems to have been esteemed one of the largest of the Fingalian giants. See Ossian agus an Clerich, v. 10. Fhir mhoir : great man or giant, &c.

There are many reasons to conclude, that these two Poems are either much interpolated, or the work of a late age. Many words, apparently derived from the English, occur in them, similar to those in the Song of the death of Dermid;* such are Bheist, Nobul, Maighdin, Mantul, Ghun, &c.

When I left Dalmaly the last time, I requested Mac-Nab to send me such Erse poems, as he might afterwards collect: in consequence of which, he inclosed a Song called Urnigh Ossian, or Ossian's Prayers, in the following letter.

"Sir,—I send you this copy of Ossian's Prayers. I could give you more now, if I had time to copy them: them I gave you was partly composed, when they went from their residence (in Cromgleann nam Cloch) that is Glenlyon Perthshire, to hunt to Ireland.—I have some good ones, I mean Poems, on Fingal's Tour to Lochlann or Denmark; wherein the Danes was defeated, and their women brought captive to Scotland—The bearer hurries me to conclude. I am, Sir, in haste,

"Your most humble servant,

"ALEX. M'NAB.

" BARCHASTAN, 27th June, 1780.
" P.S.—Please to write if they overtake you."

In this letter, Mac-Nab seems to imply that the Fingalians divided their time between Ireland and Scotland; though the Songs themselves mention only Eriu or Ireland, its peculiarities and traditions. The following Song called Ossian's Prayers, which indeed is in many respects the most curious of any, is also the only one he gave me that mentions Scotland or Allabinn. He however related to me the History of another Song; a copy of which has been published by Smith in his *Galic Antiquities,*† under the title of *The Fall of Tura;* likewise mentioning Scotland, and containing some other remarkable particulars: on which account I shall take the liberty of inserting it. It differs in many circumstances from the narrative in Smith; though the leading events are similar.

The people of Fingal, according to Mac-Nab, being on some excursion, a villain called Garrell‡ took the opportunity to set fire to one of their castles, of which it seems they had many in different places. This castle stood in the isle of Skye, and their women were confined in it: "for," said Mac-Nab, "they kept many women like the Turks." The castle being burnt down by this means, the women, unable to escape, were all destroyed together. The Fingalians were at that time sailing on the coast, and saw the fire: but though they used all the speed in their power, they arrived too late to prevent the mischief.

The above story, thus simply related by Mac-Nab, agrees with what he says in his letter about the Danish women being brought captive to Scotland by the Fingalians; and with the known manners of barbarous nations. It does not so well agree with the representation of Macpherson and Smith. §

---

* See p. 15.
† See pp. 13 and 14, where this work has been already quoted.
‡ Smith calls this man Gara; and makes him one of Fingal's heroes, who was left at home as a guard when the accident happened.
§ See p. 15 and note.

Glenlyon, which Mac-Nab in his letter speaks of, as one of the principal abodes of the Fingalians, lies in the western part of Perthshire, on the borders of Argyleshire, near Loch-Tay.

Throughout this country are many ruins of rude stone walls, constructed in a circle; the stones of which are very large : these are said by tradition to be the work of Fingal and his heroes. One of these ruins is close by Mac-Nab's house. The Pictish houses are buildings of this sort.

Many places in the country, as glens, lochs, islands, &c. are denominated from the Fingalians. The largest cairns, which abound here, are said to be their sepulchral monuments : indeed all striking objects of nature, or great works of rude and ancient art, are attributed to them; as other travellers have already informed the world. The zeal of Fingalianism has, however, in one instance, bestowed these titles improperly. The great cave of Staffa, which Sir Joseph Banks calls Fingal's Cave, is, by the inhabitants, called *The Cave of Twilight.* The Erse word for twilight is similar to the sound of Fingal ; and hence proceeded the error.

I am sorry to add, that Mac-Nab never sent me any more Songs after the Urnigh Ossian; though I wrote him an answer, requesting that he would favour me with any others he pleased : and urged every persuasive to obtain them. Money is little used, and therefore little esteemed, in the Highlands of Scotland.

Barchastan, from whence he dates his letter, is the name of the house he lives at, in the parish of Dalmaly in Glenorchy.

The following Song, called Urnigh Ossian, or Ossian's Prayers, is the relation of a dispute between Ossian and St. Patrick, on the evidence and excellence of Christianity. The arguments of St. Patrick are by no means those of an able Polemic : but the objections of Ossian carry with them the internal marks of antiquity : they are evidently the objections of a rude Polytheist, totally ignorant of the nature of the Christian tenets ; and such as no later bards in such a rude country would ever have been able to invent, without some original and traditional foundation. Ossian seems to have thought, that hell might be as agreeable as heaven, if there were as many deer and dogs in it. "Why," says Ossian, "should I be religious, if heaven be not in the possession of Fingal and his Heroes? I prefer them to thy God, and thee, O Patrick!" So Purchas relates,* that, when the Spaniards attempted to convert the inhabitants of the Philippine isles to Christianity; the Islanders replied, that they would rather be in hell with their forefathers, than in heaven with the Spaniards.

According to Mac-Nab, Fingal seems to have been the Odin of the Scots : for he said, they had no religion, prior to Christianity, but the reverence of Fingal and his race. This account agrees with the entire deficiency of religious ideas, in the Ossian of Macpherson and Smith; and with the opinions and prejudices expressed in the following Poem, and in some of the foregoing.†

The Urnigh Ossian evidently appears, even through the medium of the following rude translation, to be superior in poetic merit to any of the Songs which accompany it. I am very sorry the translation is not entire. The first twenty-one verses, and the last verse, or thirty-sixth, were translated for me

* Pilgrimage Asia Ch. 16.
† See p. 7, v. 4.

at Oban in Argyleshire, by a schoolmaster there; who was procured by Mr. Hugh Stephenson, inn-keeper, at Oban. The remainder of the translation was sent me from Edinburgh, in consequence of Dr. Willan's application.* I wish some of your readers, Mr. Urban, could be induced to supply the deficiency.

URNIGH OSSIAN.

1.

AITHRIS sgeula Phadruig
An onair do Leibhigh
'Bheil neamh gu harrid
Aig Uaisliamh na Féinne.

2.

Bheirinnsa mo dheurbha dhuil
Oishein nau glonn
Nach bheil Neamh aig t athair
Aig Oscar no aig Goll.

3.

'Sdona'n sgéula Phadruig
'La agad damhsa Chlerich
Com'am bothinnsa ri cràbha
Mur bheil Neamh aig Flaith no Fhéinne

4.

Nach dona sin Oishein
Fhir nam briathra boille
Gum b'fhear Dia ri 'sgacto aon' chàs
Na Fiànïn Allabinn Uille

V. 1.

RELATE the tale of Patrick, in honour of your ancestors.—" Is heaven on high in the possession of the Heroes of Fingal?

ST. PATRICK. **2.**

I assure thee, O Ossian! father of many children † that heaven is not in the possession of thy father, nor of Oscar, nor of Gaul. ‡

OSSIAN. **3.**

It is a pitiful tale, O Patrick! that thou tellest me the Clerk of: Why should I be religious, if Heaven be not in the possession of the heroes of Fingal?

ST. PATRICK. **4.**

How wicked is that, O Ossian! thou who usest blasphemous expressions: God is much more mighty than all the Heroes of Albion.

* See p. 17.

† This is ever accounted a great honour among Barbarians. See also Ossian agus an Clerich, v. 47, p. 12.

‡ I copied at Mac-Nab's, out of one of his MSS. the following lines, relative to Gaul abovementioned, which relate an incident remarkably similar to the stories told of Achilles, Hercules, the Jewish Samson, and the Teutonic giant Thor, &c. I observed in p. 18, that Gaul is generally esteemed one of the greatest of the giants: this extract describes one still mightier than he.

Cho drugain mo sgian do riogh na do Fhlath
No do dhuin air bith gun amhith no mhath
Naoid guinuiran do sgun achuire anansa Goull
'Scho n fhuigin a thri annan biodh mo sgian nam dhonr
Ach dom gan tug luthadh lamh-ada ananccan Ghuill anathadh
Gheig² e rann bhris e enai geal anceaumhum hom a mhi lean ta
Chuir cmhala farascal mhaoidh eain adheud rum h'or
Chuir e falam hors aghuiudhi agus enig me air na truighe
Sb'huin adhann don tallamh 'sgula bhath belhidh fhaiil 'ann
Farnach deanadh andan ach ball gorm na glas
So ruda dheanadh an sgian an riach sanrrachadh abhor.

The sense of these lines, Mac-Nab gave me as follows: "Gaul and Uvavat had a violent conflict: Gaul had a knife, Uvavat had none: Gaul stabbed Uvavat nine times with his knife: Uvavat said, if he had had his knife, he would not have suffered a third part so much; at last, lifting up his arm, he struck Gaul on the skull, and fractured it; broke his bone; removed his brow; knocked out his teeth; knocked off his kneepan and his five toes; all at one blow. The mark of the blow shall remain in the ground for ever." Gaul's knife mentioned here seems to have been a kind of dirk; which, like the dagger of Hudibras, served in these rude times,

Either for fighting, or for drudging;
And when 't had stabb'd, or broke a head;
It would scrape trenchers, or chip bread.

5.

Bfhearr leam aon' Chath laidir
'Churieadh Fiunn na Féinne
Na Tighearnagh achrabhidh sin
Is tusa Chléirich.

OSSIAN. **5.**

I would prefer one mighty battle, fought
by the Heroes of Fingal, to the God of thy
worship, and thee, O Clerk.

6.

Ga beag a Chubhail chrobhnanach
Is mònaran na Gréine
Gun fhios don Riogh mhòrdhalach
Cha drèid fieidh dhile do Sgéithe

ST. PATRICK. **6.**

Little as is the *Chubhail*, or the sound of
Greini: yet it is as well known to this
Almighty King as the least of your shields.*

7.

'Noavil ù'm bionan e s mac Cubhall
An Riogh sin a bha air na F annibh
Dhéfheudadh fir an domhain
Dol na Fhallamhian gun iaruidh.

OSSIAN. **7.**

Dost thou imagine that he is equal to
the son of Comhal? that King who reigned
over the nations, who defeated all the
people of the earth, and visited their
kingdoms unsent for!†

8.

Oishain 'sfada do shuain
Eirieh suas is eist na 'Sailm
Chaill a do lùth sdo ràth
Scho chuir u cath ri la garbh

ST. PATRICK. **8.**

O thou Ossian! long sleep has taken hold
of thee: rise to hear the Psalms! Thou hast
lost thy strength and thy valour, neither
shalt thou be able to withstand the fury of
the day of battle.

9.

Mo chail mi mo lùth smo ràth
'Snach mairionn cath abh'aig Fiunn
Dod chleirs neachd sa's beag mo spéis
'S Do chiol eisteachd chonfheach leom

OSSIAN. **9.**

If I have lost my strength and my valour,
and none of Fingal's battles be remembered;
I will never pay respect to thy Clerkship,
nor to thy pitiful songs.

10.

Chachualas co meath mo cheòil
O thùs an domhain mhoir gus anochd
Tha ri aosta annaghleochd liath
Thir a dhioladh Cliar air chnochd

ST. PATRICK. **10.**

Such beautiful songs as mine were never
heard till this night.‡ O thou who hast
discharged many a sling§ upon the hills!
though thou art old and unwise.

11.

'Strie a dhiol mi cliar air chnochd
'Illephadreig is Olc rùn
'Seacoir dhuitsa chàin mo chruth
Onach dfhuair u guth air thùs.

OSSIAN. **11.**

Often have I discharged many a sling,§
upon a hill, O thou Patrick of wicked mind!
In vain dost thou endeavour to reform me,
as thou first hast been appointed to do it.

12.

Chualas Ceol Oscionn do cheòil
Ge mòr a mholfas tu do Chliar
Ceòl air nach luigh leatrom laoich
Faoghar cuile aig an Ord Thiànn

12.

Music we have heard that exceeds thine,
though thou praisest so much thy hymns;
songs which were no hindrance to our
heroes; the noble songs of Fingal.

---

* This verse appears to be erroneously translated; the translator said, he knew not
how to render the words Chubhail and Greine properly: the third verse also, in which
Ossian is called the Clerk, a title, commonly given to St. Patrick, and some few other
parts, seem not altogether correct.

† I suspect the expressions translated by Macpherson, *The Kings of the World,* are
somewhat similar to these. Fingal is here represented as a Bacchus or Sesostris.

‡ This seems to refer to the custom of singing songs at night, a favourite entertainment
of the Highlands perhaps to this day. In v. 8, Ossian seems to be represented as falling
asleep, instead of listening to St. Patrick.

§ The word Cliar, here translated a sling, may perhaps mean some other weapon.

13.

'Nuair a Shuig headh Fiunn air chnochd
Sheinneneid port don Ord fhiann
Chuire nan codal na Slòigh
'S Ochòin ba bhinue na do Chliar

13.

When Fingal sat upon a hill, and sung a tune to our heroes, which would enchant the multitude to sleep: Oh! how much sweeter was it than thy hymns.*

14.

Smeorach bheag dhuth o Ghleann smàil
Faghar nom bàre rie an tuinn
Sheinnemid fein le' puirt
'Sbha sinn feinn sair Cruitt ro bhinn

14.

Sweet are the thrush's notes, and lovely the sound of the rushing waves against the side of the bark ; but sweeter far the voice of the harps, when we touched them to the sound of our songs.

15.

Bha bri gaothair dheug aig Fiunn
Zugradhmed cad air Ghleann smàil
'Sbabhenne Glaoghairm air còn
Na do chlaig a Cleirich chàidh

15.

Frequently we heard the voices of our Heroes among the hills and glens ; and more sweet to our ears was the noise of our hounds, than thy bells, O Clerk ! †

16.

Coid arinn Fiunn air Dia
A reir do Chliar is do scoil
Thug e la air pronnadh Oir
San athlo air meoghair Chon.

16.

Was Fingal created to serve God, to please the Clerk and his school ?‡ he who has been one day distributing § gold, and another following the toes of dogs.

17.

Aid miadt fhiughair ri meoghair chon
'Sri diolagh scol gaeb aon la
'Sgun eisheamail thoirt do Dhia
'Nois tha Fiunn nan Fiaunun laimh

St. Patrick. 17.

As much respect as thou payest to the toes of dogs, and to discharge thy daily school :‖ Yet because thou hast not paid respect to God, thou and the heroes of thy race shall be led captive in Hell.

18.

Sgann achreideas me do sgéul
A Chléirich led leabhar bàn
Gum bithidh Fiunn na chomh fhial
Aig Duine no aig Dia an laimh

Ossian. 18.

I can hardly believe thy tale, thou light-haired and unworthy Clerk !¶ that the Heroes of our race should be in captivity, either to the Devil or to God.

19.

Ann an Ifrionn tha én laimh
Fear lin sath bhi pronnadh Oir
Air son a dhio mios air Dia
Chuirse e'n tighpian fuidh Chrou

St. Patrick. 19.

He is now bound in Hell, who used to distribute gold. Because he was a despiser of God, he has Hell for his portion.

---

* When the Bards sung their songs at night, it seems to have been their custom to pursue them, till they had lulled their audience to sleep : See v. 10 and note : which accounts for the singular effect here attributed to Fingal's Songs. It is related of Alfarabi, whom Abulfeda and Ebn Khalecan call the greatest Philosopher of the Mussulmans, that being at the Court of Seifeddoula Sultan of Syria, and requested to exhibit some of his Poems, he produced one, which he sung to an accompanyment of several instruments. The first part of it threw all his audience into a violent laughter, the second part made them all cry, and the last lulled even the performers to sleep. Herb. Dict. Orient in voce. Thus also Mercury is said to have lulled Argus to sleep by music.

† Ossian agrees with modern hunters, in his idea of the musick of a pack of hounds. The bells mentioned in this verse appear to be an interpolation.

‡ "And Pharaoh said, Who is Jehovah that I should obey his voice to let Israel go ? I know not Jehovah." Exod. v. 2.

§ The word in the original signifies pounding gold : it occurs again in v. 19.

‖ What school did Ossian keep ?

¶ Why was light hair esteemed an opprobrium ? the Erse themselves are a red-haired race.

20.

Nam bithidh Clanna' Morn' asteach
'S Clann Oboigé nam fear lréun
Bheiremid ne Fiunn amach
No bhiodh an teach aguinn séin

If the children of Morni, and the many tribes of the children of Ovi, were yet alive ; we would force the brave Fingal out of Hell, or the habitation should be our own. *

21.

Cionfheodhna na Halabinn maseach
Air leatsa gum ba mhor am féum
Cho dtuga fin Fiunn amach
Ged bhiodh an teach aguibhfein

Valiant as you imagine the brave Scots were ; yet Fingal they would not release, though they should be there themselves.

22.

Coid an tait Joghairne fein
Aphadruig a léib has an scoil
Nach co math's Flathinnis De
Ma Gheibhar ann Fcigh is Coin

What place is that same Hell, Patrick of deep learning ! Is it not as good as the Heaven of God, if hounds and deer are found there ? †

23.

Bha mise la air Sliabh boid
Agus Coilte ba chruaigh lann
Bha Oscar ann 's Goll nan Sliagh
Donall nam fleagh s ròn on Ghleann

24.

Fiunn mac Cubhill borb abhriogh
Bha e na Rioghos air ceann
Tri mic ar Riogh os na n sgia
Ba m hor amian air dol a Shealg.
Sa phadruig naun bachoil fiàl
Cho leigeadh iad Dia os an ceann

24.

Fingal the son of Comhal, fierce in action, was King over us. To the three sons of the King of Shields, pleasant was the chace. Generous Patrick of the innocent staff ! they would never permit God to be named as their superior.‡

25.

Ba bheach leam Dearmad e duibhn
Agus Fearagus ba bhinne Glòir
Nam ba chead leal mi efa n luaidh
A Chleirich nuadh a theid don roim

25.

Much rather would I speak of Dermid, and Duino, and Fergus of eloquent speech, if you would give me leave to mention them, O holy man who goest to Rome.§

26.

Com nach ocad leam u dun luaidh
Ach thoir aire gu luath air Dia
'Nois tha deireadh air tòis
'Scuir do d Chaois ashean fhirlé

Why should I not permit you to mention them ? but take care to make mention of God. Now the last things are become first. Change thou therefore thy ways, old man with the grey locks. ‖

* The Greek stories about the visit of Hercules to Hell, for the purpose of delivering Theseus and fetching up Cerberus, are strikingly similar to the idea of this verse.

† Mac-Nab mentioned this verse and the thirty-sixth when I saw him : for he had spoken to me about this poem before he sent it.

‡ Though Ossian is generally represented as the son of Fingal, this verse and the next do not seem to speak of him in that relation. Mac-Nab said St. Patrick was Fingal's son. See also p. 7.

§ The contest here considerably resembles that at the beginning of *Ossian agus an Clerich*, (see p. 7 as above). The Roman Catholic superstition of later times in this passage evidently discovers itself : perhaps the *innocent staff*, mentioned in v. 24, may have some reference to the crosier.

‖ St. Patrick, Jesuit-like, seems willing to compound with Ossian ; and to admit the Pagan songs, provided Ossian, on the other hand, would admit Christianity. Part of this verse is scriptural, " *So the last shall be first and the first last, for many are called but few chosen.*" Matt. xx. 16. and see also Mark ix. 35. Jesus Christ is here meant by the title of God : See verse 28.

27.

Phadruig mathug u ccad beagann
Alabhairt duirn
Nach aidmhich ñunas cead le Dia
Flath nan fiann arait' air thus

28.

Cho d tug mise comas duit
Sheanfhir chursta is tu liath
B'fhear Mac moire ri aon lo
No duine dtaineg riamh

29.

Nir raibh math aig neach fuin 'Ghrèin
Gum bfhear efèin na mo thrialh
Mac muirneach nach d'eittich Cliar
Scha leige se Dia osachian

30.

Na comh'ad 'usa Duine ri Dia
Sheann fhir le na breathnich e
'S fada on thainig aneart
'Smairfidh se leart Gu brath

31.

'Chomhad innse Fuinn namsleagh
Ri aon neach asheall sa Ghrein
Cha d carr se riamh ne air neach
'Scho mho dhearr se niach ma ni

32.

'S bheiremid seachd cath a fichead an fhiann
Air Shithair druim a Cliar amuidh
'Scho d tugamid Urram do Dhia
No chean cliar abha air bith

33.

Seachd catha fichiad duibhs nar fein
Cho do chreid sibh ne n Dia nan Dùl
Cho mhairionn duine dar Sliochd
Scho bheo ach riochd Oishein Uir

34.

Cha ne fin ba choireach ruinn
Acts Turish Fhinn a dhol don Roimh
Cumail Cath Gabhridh ruinn feir
Bha e Claoidh bhur fèin ro mhor

35

Chone Chlaoidhsibh Uille fhann
Amhu Fhinnos gearr gud re
Eist ri rà Riogh nam bochd
Iar thusa 'nachd neamh dheul fein.

36.

Comracch an da Abstaildeùg
Gabham chugam feir aniugh
Ma rinn mise Peacadh trom
Chuir an cnochd sa n tòm sa'nluig.

BARCHASTAN GLENORCHY, *June* 27, 1780.

OSSIAN. 27.
Patrick, since thou hast given me leave
to speak a little, wilt thou not permit us,
with God's leave, to mention the King of
Heroes first ? *

ST. PATRICK. 28.
I by no means give thee leave, thou
wicked grey-haired man ! The son of the
virgin Mary is more excellent than any
man who ever appeared upon earth.

30.
Compare not any to God ; harbour no
such thoughts, old man ! Long has his
superior power stood acknowledged, and it
shall for ever continue.

OSSIAN. 31.
I certainly would compare the hospitable
Fingal to any man who ever looked the sun in
the face. He never asked a favour of another,
nor did he ever refuse when asked.†

OSSIAN. 36.
The belief of the twelve Apostles I now
take unto me : and if I have sinned greatly,
let it be thrown into the grave.
CRIOCH.

---

* The opposition of Ossian seems to be considerably weakened in this verse : but he
still wishes to see his old superstitions maintain the superiority at least.

† Ossian seems to have been offended at the gross reproaches which the humility of
the Christian Apostle had just bestowed upon him with all the prodigality of one of
Homer's heroes : and he answers with the rough but generous boldness of barbarous
independence.

I shall conclude these Erse songs, with a Poem called the Ode of Oscar; whose authenticity perhaps admits the least Dispute of any which I have sent you. I did not obtain it, like most of the rest, from Mac-Nab; but wrote it down immediately from the mouth of a Man who was Wright or Carpenter at Mr. Macleane's of Drumnan in Morven, and who knew a number of these songs. Mrs. Macleane and her son's wife, a daughter of Sir Alexander Macleane, were so kind as to sit by and translate for me whilst he repeated and I wrote. In order to have some kind of check against deception, I attempted to write down the Erse, together with the translation; but as a language, written by one who is a stranger to it, must necessarily be unintelligible, I shall only trouble you with the latter. The poem relates the Death of Oscar; which is the subject of the first book of Macpherson's Temora. It opens with a lamentation for the Death of Chaoilte, which is foreign to the rest of the song; a practice not uncommon among the poems attributed to Ossian, and similar to that of Pindar. I do not remember to have met with the name of Chaoilte in Macpherson or Smith; but it has already been twice mentioned in the foregoing songs: in Cubha Fhinn, line 27, and Urnigh Ossian, verse 23.

1.

I AM very sad after thee, Chaoilte! since those who were my contemporaries are departed. I am filled with Grief, Sorrow, and Pain, since my foster-brother is gone from me.*

2.

Chaoilte, my dear foster-brother! I would fight under thy banners in all weathers: Chaoilte! thou wert my support in times of success and honour.

3.

Did you hear of Fingal's journeys on every forest in Erin? Great Cairbar with his armour sent for us to destroy us.†

4 and 5.

We were not all of us about the house that were able to satisfy him: but nine score of noble riders, on great grey horses. We got honour and respect as we at all times acquired; but we got still more than that Comhal and Cairbar pursuing us.‡

6.

The last day of our drinking match, Cairbar spoke with his tremendous voice: "I want we should exchange arms, brown Oscar that comest from Albion.§

OSCAR. **7.**

What exchange do you want to make, great Cairbar, who even press the Ships into your service; and to whom I and all my host belong, in time of war and battle?‖

---

* The intimate connection of fosterage here so strongly expressed is in a great degree peculiar to Ireland, and seems strongly to point out the origin of this song.

† This verse exactly agrees with the narrative of Macpherson.

‡ These verses are by no means consonant to the poems of Macpherson. Riding is a practice unknown in them: his heroes are all charioteers. The Comhal of Macpherson also is the father of Fingal; whereas he is here united with Cairbar, Fingal's greatest foe.

§ The quarrel in Macpherson begins after a treacherous feast, though not of so long duration as that here referred to. Cairbar in Macpherson does not desire Oscar to exchange, but to surrender his spear. "Oscar, said the dark red Cairbar, I behold the spear of Erin. The spear of Temora glitters in thy hand, son of Woody Morven!—Yield it, son of Ossian!—Yield it to carborne Cairbar!"—Temora Book I.

‖ "Shall I yield, Oscar replied, the gift of Erin's insured King, &c." The reply of Oscar in the poem above by no means agrees with Macpherson, it even seems to represent Oscar as a vassal of Cairbar.

8.

Surely it is oppression to demand our heads when we have not arms to defend ourselves. The reason of your doing so is our being deprived of Fingal and his Son.

9.

Were Fingal and my Father with us as they used to be, you would not during your whole life obtain the breadth of your feet in Erin.*

10.

The great hero (Cairbar) was filled with rage at the dispute which arose between them. There were exceeding horrible words between Cairbar and Oscar.

11.

That night the women had a warm dispute about the heroes, and even Cairbar and Oscar themselves were half and half angry.†

12.

Nine score men armed with Bows and Arrows, that came to destroy us; all these fell by the hand of Oscar enraged at the sons of Ireland.‡

13.

Nine score strong able Irishmen, that came bounding over the rough highland seas; all these fell by the hand of Oscar enraged at the sons of Ireland.‡

14.

Nine score brave sons of Albion, that came from rude and distant climes; all these fell by the hand of Oscar enraged at the sons of Ireland.‡

15.

When the red-haired Cairbar saw Oscar destroying his people, he threw his Javelin dipt in poison at Oscar.§

16.

Oscar fell on his right knee, and the poisoned Javelin pierced through his heart: but before he expired, he struck a mortal blow, that killed the king of Erin.‖

17.

Fingal addressed his grandson and said, " Do you remember the dreadful battle we fought on Ben-Erin? You were sorely wounded on that day, yet you were cured by my hand.¶

18.

Oscar replied to his grandfather. "My cure is not under the heavens; for Cairbar plunged his Javelin, dipt in poison, between my Navel and my Reins.**

19.

And there was great slaughter that day by the hand of Oscar: he slew Cairbar at one blow, and his son Arsht that great hero at the next.††

20.

We bore the corpse of the beautiful Oscar, sometimes on our shoulders, and sometimes on our Javelins. We carried him in the most respectful manner to the hall of his grand-father. ‡‡

---

* "Were he who fought with little men (Fingal), near Atha's haughty chief (Cairbar), Atha's chief would yield green Erin to avoid his rage."

† What night is this? What have these Women to do with the dispute? There is no appearance of these circumstances in Macpherson. I suspect there is some omission in this part of the poem.

‡ The original I believe represents Oscar as a Giant, and as killing these multitudes at one stroke. The title of Great Hero given to Cairbar v. 10, and to Arst v. 19, I believe means also Giant in the Erse. See likewise Ossian agus an Clerich v. 10 and Note on the Cubha Fhinn, p. 18, about Gaul.—I do not understand why Irishmen are represented in v. 12, as bounding over the highland seas to Ireland.—'Behold, says Macpherson, they fall before Oscar like groves in the desert, when an angry ghost rushes through night, and takes their green heads in his hand. Morlath falls, Maronnan dies, Conachar trembles in his blood."

§ "*Dark red Cairbar.*" See note § on v. 6. Macpherson does not mention poison. "Cairbar shrinks before Oscar's sword. He creeps in darkness behind a stone; he lifts the spear in secret, and pierces Oscar's side."

‖ "Oscar falls forward on his shield: his knee sustains the chief. But still his spear is in his hand. See gloomy Cairbar falls."

¶ How came Fingal to his Grandson? there seems to have been an omission in this place also.—Fingal is the Machaon of his army here, as in the song of the death of Dermid. See p. 14, and note ‡.

** The wound is described here with all the particularity of Homer.

†† Arsht is not mentioned by Macpherson. See also note ‡ on verses 12, 13, 14, above.

‡‡ Fingal is evidently represented here as living in Ireland in spite of v. 6, and verses 12, 13, and 14. Macpherson transports the corpse by sea to Morven.

21.

And Oscar said, The howlings of my own dogs, and the cries of the old heroes, with the dreadful lamentation of the women, grieve me more than the pain I feel from the poisoned Javelin.*

22.

Such were the distresses of the multitude for Oscar, that even the women forgot to grieve for their own husbands, or their brothers, as all that surrounded the house were mourning for Oscar.†

23.

Fingal said, " Thou wert my son, and the son of my son. Thou wert my love, and the love of my son. My heart beats sore at thy untimely end : it galls me to the soul that Oscar is no more.‡

24.

It was never imagined by any person that your heart was made of any other materials than steel.§

25.

Oscar, the son of my lucky beloved Ossian, raised the vast flag from off the head of the King ; which was the last brave action of the hero.||

Mr. Macpherson in a note on his Temora¶ mentions an Irish Poem on this subject, which he had seen ; and wherein the death of Oscar is related with many different circumstances. The quarrel is indeed ascribed to a dispute at a feast, about the exchange of arms : but it does not represent the Heroes as fighting, till some time after, upon Cairbar's meeting Oscar at the Pass of Gabhhra, through which Oscar was returning home with the spoils of Ireland, which he had been ravaging in consequence of the quarrel. Possibly Mr. Macpherson might say, the foregoing poem also is Irish ; and indeed not without reason, notwithstanding it contains some of the very passages he has inserted in his Temora.

Since I sent you the two untranslated Poems, called Duan a Mhuileartich and Cubha Fhinn, p. 17 and 18, I have received the following account of their contents, in consequence of Dr. Willan's application to his friends at Edinburgh. The first of them, or the *Duan a Mhuileartich*, is " an account

---

* When Oscar, says Macpherson, saw his friends around, his " heaving breast arose. The groans, he said, of aged chiefs, the howling of my dogs, the sudden bursts of the song of grief, have melted Oscar's soul : my soul that never melted before." The dogs are here represented as feeling a very extraordinary sympathy with the passions of the human race, a property they perhaps might acquire, by their perpetual communion with men in a savage state.

† " And they did weep, O Fingal ! dear was the hero to their souls — No father mourned his son slain in youth : no brother his brother of love.—They fell without tears, for the chief of the people was low."

‡ Fingal in Macpherson says, " Art thou fallen, O Oscar, in the midst of thy course : the heart of the aged bears over thee.—Weep ye heroes of Morven, never more shall Oscar rise, &c."

§ Oscar in Macpherson thus speaks of himself : " My soul that never melted before, it was like the steel of my sword." See the note on v. 21.

|| Mrs. Macleane, jun. to whose elegant abilities and hospitable friendship I was principally indebted for the foregoing song, honoured me with the traditional explication of this verse, which is in the true style of gigantic fable. It agrees with Macpherson, in respect to Cairbar's hiding himself in a hole, when he attacked Oscar (see the note on v. 15) ; and represents Oscar as possessing an invulnerability, very similar to that of Achilles and Orlando.—" The word flag, here used, relates to the following story : Oscar could only be slain by his own javelin : This Cairbar knew when he desired to exchange arms with him. After Cairbar had slain Oscar with his javelin, he hid himself in a hole of the earth, and covered himself with an enormous flag, which is above referred to."—Perhaps, however, the last verse affords some suspicion, that it is in itself an interpolation.

¶ B. I. p. 14. edit. 8vo, 1773.

of a hideous monster called Muilcartich, which swam by sea into Ireland, attacked Fingal's army, killed a number of his men, and was at last killed by his own hand." I ardently wish that this remarkable poetical romance was literally translated, as it probably may contain much curious knowledge. It strikingly resembles the serpent of Bagrada, which is said to have opposed the Roman army under Regulus, in Africa.

The first part of the other Poem, called *Cubha Fhinn do Riogh Lochlin*, describes " the compensation offered by Fingal to the King of Lochlin, to save Ireland from a threatened invasion.

"A thousand whelps; a thousand dogs;
A thousand collars * upon a thousand dogs;
A thousand spears fit for battle; †
A thousand fine plaids of the brightest colours; ‡
A thousand hardy bay horses; §
A thousand nobles of red gold;
A thousand maidens with two gowns; ||

A thousand mantles of new silk; ¶
A thousand warriors wearing them;
A thousand bridles of gold and silver.
"Though the King of Lochlin should get these things, and all the wealth of Ireland, he and his people would not return back, till Ireland should be tributary to them." **

The remainder of this Poem is a description of the standards of Fingal's army, as they appeared in order. Perhaps this part may contain some of the passages of Mr. Macpherson's Ossian.

It is already observed, that these Poems evidently appear to attribute Fingal to Ireland, †† an assertion which the foregoing account of these two Poems so strongly corroborates, that I could not omit repeating it here.

I shall trouble you, Gentlemen, with another letter of conclusions, deducible as they appear to me, from the foregoing premises, but which I shall endeavour to render as concise as possible. I esteem myself much indebted to you for the attention you have already shewn, to,

GENTLEMEN,

Your very humble servant,

THO. F. HILL.

ELY-PLACE, HOLBORN.

* Or *Chains to lead them.*
† Or *Lochaber Axes.*
‡ Or *fine wool or silk coverings.*
§ Or hard red breast plates.
|| Such maidens were probably scarce. See also p. 19, about the customs relating to women.
¶ See p. 8, v. 9.
** Mac-Nab translated part of this poem for me; yet tho' he wrote the copy of it, he did not seem clearly to understand it.
†† See p. 19.

CONCLUSION OF THE REMARKS ON OSSIAN.

I. *Of the Evidence afforded by the foregoing Poems, that there are Songs traditionally preserved in the Highlands and attributed to Ossian ; containing Parts of the Poems, published by Mr.* Macpherson *and Mr.* Smith, *under the name of that Bard.*

II. *Of the Authenticity of the* Ossian *of* Macpherson *and* Smith : *how far it is founded upon the Highland Songs ; and how far those Songs may be regarded as the real Works of* Ossian.

III. *Of the Country of* Ossian, *whether he was an Highlander or an Irishman ?*

IV. *Of the real Character of* Ossian *and the* Fingalians, *and who they probably were.*

I.

IT is evident, Mr. Urban, from the collection of Erse Poems which I have sent you, that there are many traditional Songs preserved in the Highlands relating to Fingal and his heroes, as well as to several other subjects. It is also evident, that these Songs contain portions of the very Poems published by Mr. Macpherson and Mr. Smith, under the name of Ossian. We may therefore justly conclude, that those Poems are not wholly the forgery of their editors, but compiled at least from original Songs.* I by no means think it worth my while, to notice the various concessions in favour of this conclusion, which the minor antagonists of Ossian have of late been forced to make. I myself have given proofs of it, which need I hope no external confirmation. To these proofs might be added, that I met with many traditional preservers of these Songs, in every different part of the Highlands : some of whom, especially in Argyleshire, Lochaber, and on the rest of the western coast, were said to possess various Poems attributed to Ossian, although I had neither leisure nor opportunity to collect copies from them.— But enough has already been said on this subject, if my testimony deserves regard.

II.

These principles being established, it remains to be considered how far the Poems, published by Macpherson and Smith, deserve to be considered as the works of Ossian.

The foregoing Songs, attributed to that bard, which contain passages of the Ossian of Macpherson and Smith, are by no means uniformly consistent with the Poems in which the parallel passages are found, but frequently relate to different events, and even contain different circumstances. From hence it seems probable, that Mr. Macpherson and Mr. Smith compiled their publications from those parts of the Highland Songs which they most approved, combining them into such forms as, according to their ideas, were most excellent, retaining the old names and the leading events.† In this process they were supported and encouraged by the variety of Songs preserved in the Highlands upon the same subject, and by the various modes in which the same event is related. Mr. Macpherson may indeed have MSS. of all the Poems he has published ; which MSS. may have been compiled by their

---

* See p. 4.   † See p. 5.

collector ; or they may possibly contain entire Poems really ancient. But Mr. Smith has honestly acknowledged, that he himself compiled his Ossian in the manner above described. "After the materials were collected," says he, "the next labour was to compare the different editions ; to strike off several parts that were manifestly spurious ; * to bring together some episodes that appeared to have a relation to one another, though repeated separately ; and restore to their proper places some incidents that seemed to have run from one Poem into another:—and hence it was unavoidably necessary to throw in sometimes a few lines or sentences to join some of the episodes together.— I am sensible that the form of these Poems is considerably altered from what is found in any one of the editions from which they are compiled. They have assumed somewhat more of the appearance of regularity and art than that bold and irregular manner, in which they are originally delivered."

Mr. Smith also speaks of the Ossian of Mr. Macpherson in a somewhat similar manner :† "That we have not the whole of the Poems of Ossian, or even of the collection translated by Mr. Macpherson, we allow ; yet still we have many of them, and of almost all a part. The building is not entire, but we have still the grand ruins of it.

What portion, therefore, of the Ossian of Macpherson and Smith is original, no man can determine except themselves. Smith indeed says, that he has mentioned all his *material* alterations, transpositions, and additions, in his notes ; and that, *for the most part*, he was guided in them by the Sgeulachds, or traditionary tales accompanying the songs : but there are few such notes in his book, and perhaps as few *such* Sgeulachds in the mouths of the Highlanders. In Macpherson and Smith also we see these Poems divested of their idiomatic peculiarities and fabulous ornaments ; which renders it impossible to discover what manners and opinions are really ancient, and what are of modern invention. Yet it is remarkable, that in spite of all the objections to their authenticity, necessarily produced by such a treatment of them, they still possess an internal evidence of originality, which has enabled them hitherto to withstand all the torrent of opposition.

The Ossian of Macpherson and Smith appears therefore to be a mutilated work ; even though we should suppose that the songs they originally compiled from were the undoubted works of that celebrated bard. But this is far from being the case ; for even allowing that an Ossian ever existed and wrote, yet time must have introduced such material changes in his works, if preserved merely by tradition during so long a period, that their own author would hardly know them again. I think it, however, doubtful, whether such a being as Ossian ever appeared in the world.

All the Songs which I met with in the Highlands, relative to the Feinne, or Fingalians, were attributed to Ossian : his name seems merely a common title, which is ascribed to all the poetic annals of his race.‡

From these considerations we seem authorised finally to conclude, that the Ossian of Macpherson and Smith is a mutilated compilation from Highland Songs, ascribed indeed to that bard, yet very little likely to be his composition. Out of these they selected the best parts, and rejected such as they thought might discredit the character of Highland antiquity ; attri-

* Such as the Chuach Fhin, &c. See pp. 14 and 15.
† Smith, Galic Antiq. pp. 123, 128 to 130.
‡ See hereafter, p. 34.

buting them to later times, and the ignorant bards of the fifteenth century. Perhaps even the works of Homer himself, which had so many different editions, very considerably varying from each other, were compiled by a somewhat similar process from the ancient Greek Songs.*

III.

Another question remains to be considered : Whether these Songs are the compositions of the Highlands or of Ireland? and, Whether Ossian was an Irish or Caledonian Scot? I have already expressed my opinion, that the Songs in this collection evidently manifest a connection with Ireland, though their traditional preservation in Scotland has sometimes introduced the name of Scotland in its stead.† One of their principal personages is St. Patrick, the peculiar Apostle of Ireland, which alone seems sufficient to mark their origin.‡ If therefore we may reason from a part to the whole, it is just to conclude, that all the other Songs preserved in the Highlands relative to the Fingalians are also Irish. They are wholly confined to the Western coast of the Highlands, opposite Ireland,§ and the very traditions of the country themselves acknowledge the Fingalians to be originally Irish. The genealogy of Fingal was there given me as follows : Fion Mac Coul, Mac Trathal, Mac Arsht Riogh Erin, or King of Ireland, thus attributing the origin of his race to the Irish. I am inclined to believe that these notions about Fingal were common to the Scots in the most ancient times, and brought by them from Ireland to Scotland, the hereditary superstition of both races; for, notwithstanding it may appear more probable that Ireland should receive colonies from Scotland than the contrary, we have direct historic evidences that Scotland received them from Ireland ; and no bare theoretic probability deserves to be opposed to the positive assertions of history.

With regard to the Erse manuscripts, about which so much has been said ; it becomes me to acknowledge, that I have never seen enough of them, to give any decided opinion : those which I have seen induce me to think, they principally owe their existence to Ireland. ||

I shall not repeat what others have said to prove the Fingalians Irish : though the connection of Fingal with Ireland has been already warmly asserted.¶

Keating, in his fabulous History of Ireland,** expressly speaks of Fion Mac Cumhail as an Irish hero, and as Commander of the Fion, a pretended body of ancient Irish Militia. He particularly mentions Fingal's jealousy of Dhiarmid Mac Dhuibne, on account of Grainé, Fingal's Wife, as represented in the songs on that subject of which I have given an account already.††

---

* See Mr. Raspe's ingenious Remarks on Ossian in his German translation of it, Blackwell's Life of Homer, &c. We have heard of a very curious MS. of Homer, discovered at Venice, containing the various readings of all the different editions. I sincerely wish the rumour may not prove fallacious.

† See pp. 7, 17, 19 and 29.

‡ The Scotch indeed lay claim to the birth of St. Patrick, and boast also his burialplace. Camden, edit. Gibson, 1695, pp. 921, 1014. And so also do the Britons, ib. p. 631, 1014. But his life and miracles all agree to attribute to Ireland.

§ See pp. 4 and 5.

|| See p. 17.

¶ See Shaw's Enquiry into the Truth of Ossian, edit. sec. p. 37, cum append, &c. O'Flaherty's Hist. of Ireland, &c. &c.

** Page 267. edit. folio, 1738.

†† See pp. 5 and 13.

But an unnoticed though curious passage in Camden affords us the most remarkable, and perhaps the most satisfactory proof that Fingal is an Irish Hero, demonstrating at least, that he was indisputably claimed by the Irish, two hundred years ago. It is contained in an extract, made by Camden, from an account of the manners of the native Irish written by one *Good*, a schoolmaster at Limerick, in 1566. "They think," says he, speaking of Ireland and its inhabitants, "the souls of the deceased are in communion with the famous men of those places, of whom they retain many stories and sonnets : as of the Giants Fin-Mac-Huyle, Osker-Mac-Osshin, or Osshin-Mac-Owim ; and they say thro' illusion that they often see them."*

IV.

The very material importance of this curious passage, with relation to the present subject, it is unnecessary to urge : for every eye must see it. We also obtain from it new information in respect to the last part of the History of Fingal and his Heroes : as it enables us to determine who they were, with a precision which must otherwise have been wanting, to complete these remarks on the Highland songs.

The singular agreement of this passage with the accounts of Ossian which were taught me in Scotland, and which I have already inserted in your Magazine, is worthy particular remark : it confirms them even in the most novel and peculiar instances. I have already given many reasons for believing that the Fingalians are generally regarded as Giants ; † but this is no novel idea : the most remarkable concurrence is in the mythologic character attributed by both to Fingal, Oscar, and Ossian. I have before remarked, that Mac-Nab described Fingal as the Odin of the Scots ; and that the song called Urnigh Ossian ‡ evidently speaks of him as such. This curious passage represents him exactly in the same character ; a Hero with whom the spirits of the deceased are in communion, who is their Chieftain, and the Lord of the Feasts. The Gods of all the Northern Nations seem to have been of this class : mighty Heroes, esteemed once to have been invincible on earth, though perhaps not ever strictly men, nor yet constantly regarded as Giants. Such are Odin, Thor, and the other Teutonic Gods ; § such are

* Camden, edit. Gibson, 1695, p. 1048, *Of the ancient and modern customs of Ireland.*—In this edition the giants are called Fin-Mac-Huyle and Osshin-Mac-Owim. In the 8vo edition, by Bishop, in 1600, and the correct folio edition of 1607, by Bishop also, they are called Fin-Mac-Huyle and Osker-Mac-Oshin. I have inserted both above, as both strongly relate to my subject. In the late English edition, of 1772, it is Osshin-Mac-Oshin. Fin-Mac-Huyle is the same with Fion-Mac-Cumhail and Fion-Mac-Coul, see pp. 4 and 5.—Camden in the same place, p. 1046, informs us, from Good, that to swear *by the hand* of any chieftain is one of the most sacred oaths among the Irish. This very oath is found in the Poem called Ossian agus an Clerich, v. 19, see before, p. 9.

† See above, p. 14, note *, *the gigantic Boar;* also pp. 18, 21, 27 and 28, &c. Irish tradition says, that Fingal, finding the stride too great from Ireland quite to Scotland, flung a handful of earth out of the county of Down into the middle of the sea, for a stepping place, which formed the Isle of Man. Our many similar stories of Giants are perhaps more ancient than is generally imagined.

‡ See p. 21 ; and the Urnigh Ossian passim.

§ The Weird Sisters of these nations were regarded in like manner as beings little superior to witches.

C

Fingal, Oscar, and the rest of the Fingalians among the antient Scots : * Such also are Hercules, Bacchus, and even Jupiter himself, with all his sons and daughters, among the original Greeks ; a people who agreed in many particulars with our own ancestors in Northern Europe. The notions entertained about ghosts, as an intermediate order of beings between men and divinities, endowed with some share of power to do evil, is also remarkably congruous with this mythology.

As Fingal was a divine Hero, so Ossian seems to have been a divine Bard. Some of the Gods of the Teutons were Bards in like manner : the God Niord and his wife Skada quarrelled in elegant verse of their own composition ;† and Odin is the relater of his own Edda.‡ Apollo, the poetic deity to Greece, likewise sung the history of his fellow deities to men on earth, as well as Orpheus his son.§ The Bards and traditional preservers of songs in Scotland and Ireland have ever been fond of ascribing all ancient poems to this Ossian, and especially those relating to his own race ; and from this cause, the poems ascribed to Ossian are become so voluminous. || The antient Egyptians had a similar custom of ascribing their works to Hermes : οι ημετεροι ωρογονοι τα αυλων της σοφιας ευρηματα αυτω ανετιθεσαν ερμου ωαντα τα οικεια συγγραμματα εποιμαζοντες, says Jamblichus, S. l. c. 1, which rendered the Hermetic writings equally voluminous. The Egyptians, who possessed the art of writing, deposited their works in the adyta of their temples ; as the Arabians deposited their poems of old in the Temple of Mecca : but because the Egyptians affixed to them no author's name, except that of Hermes ; to him, as to the Scottish Ossian, almost all the national literature was attributed by religious flattery.

I sincerely wish, that some gentleman possessed of adequate abilities and acquaintance with the Erse language, would undertake to collect these Ossianic songs in their simple original state, as they undoubtedly contain much curious knowledge, accumulated in the various ages through which they have descended to us, and would probably afford much new information on subjects at present very ill understood. I own, however, that I should rather chuse to seek for them in Ireland than in Scotland : but neither country should be unexplored.

After having thus freely, though I hope not uncandidly, delivered my sentiments on the Ossian of Mr. Macpherson, it becomes me to acknowledge myself deeply indebted to it for the pleasure its perusal has frequently afforded me. I am willing, and indeed happy, thus publickly to declare myself a warm admirer of it as a literary composition. The novelty of its manner, of its ideas, and of the objects it describes, added to the strength and brilliancy of genius which frequently appears in it, have enabled me to read it with more delight, and to return to it more frequently, than almost any other work of modern times. And, let it be regarded in what light it

---

* As Hengist, Horsa, and the other Saxon Chiefs, derived their pedigree from Odin, so the Campbells, &c. derive their's from Dermid and the rest of the Fingalians. See above, p. 14. Thus likewise the Grecian Chieftains claimed their descent from Jupiter and his children.

† Edda, fab. 12, from Mallet's North. Antiq. Eng. trans. edit. 1770, Vol. II. pp. 71, 309, fab. 13.

‡ Ibid. pp. 3, 6, 82.   § Virg. Eclog. VI. v. 82, 83. || See before, p. 31.

may, the praise of elegant selection and composition certainly belongs to the editor. If I had not entertained these opinions of its merit, I should never have taken so much pains to investigate its authenticity; nor indeed can I believe, if the general opinion had not concurred with mine, that the world would ever have wasted so much time in disputing about it.

I cannot conclude without confessing the obligation I am under to the inhabitants of Scotland for the hospitality with which I was received by them, though a perfect stranger to much the greatest part of those who conferred such civilities upon me. If the Highlands are not distinguished for their fertility, their wealth, or the abundance of the elegancies of life, they are at least conspicuous for the generous friendship of the inhabitants, and for the performance of that benevolent Christian injunction, *Be not forgetful to entertain the stranger.* Such a reception necessarily induced me to think the best I could of their country, though it does not seem to have produced this effect upon some who had passed through it before me. I was indeed too fond of truth to shut my eyes against conviction; but I came away desirous to consider Scotland in its best point of view, although not anxious to believe in second sight.

Yours, &c.

THO. F. HILL.

ELY PLACE, *July* 10.

LORIMER AND GILLIES, PRINTERS, CLYDE STREET, EDINBURGH.